ROSEWOOD

AJ LANGE

WISH HOUSE PUBLISHING CO.

PROLOGUE

October 19, 1813

The water rose. It seeped over the banks, innocuous at first, a soft, rolling plunder, covering the exposed roots of the trees, climbing higher, encasing the ground moss and wet, damp sponge of earth that surrounded the river-fed waterway, until it lapped in gentle waves at the edge of the fields.

The workers moved quickly in the lashing rain, frantic eyes shining in the light of the remaining oil-fed torches, whites clear and stark against sweat-stained skin. Lightning pierced the dark at regular intervals, the roar of the wind eclipsing the deep rumble of thunder.

The water was coming.

It was brackish, green and brown, the bayou, and it stank of rotting leaves and wet clay and death. As it pulsed across the cotton fields, gobbling up the ground in its path, its dank stench permeated the air.

The bayou was swallowing the world.

"SIR, THE STORM." Mr. Jameson held his hat in his hand, drenched and dripping on the marble foyer as he faced his employer.

Everett Blackburn frowned at the dirty puddle that had gathered at Jameson's feet, wincing when a thunderclap shook the glass in the fanlight above the door. "Have they finished loading the barge?"

Jameson's lips thinned; Mr. Blackburn was a fair man, but a shrewd business owner. And Rosewood Manor was a business. Since moving his family onto the unblemished, fertile landscape east of the Ouachita River, the plantation owner had steadily extended his holdings until Rosewood now encompassed a vast area along the horseshoe twists and turns of the bayou Barthélémy. He had recognized the suitability of the land for growing cotton and reaped the rewards for his intuitive instincts; Rosewood was the largest cotton plantation north of Fort Miro.

"The barge is on it's way, but the ship should remain at port until the storm passes," Jameson said quietly.

"They will sail tonight." Everett lifted his gaze to the curved staircase where his daughter Emmeline stood, clutching a finely turned spindle, eyes widening with each deafening clap of thunder. He turned to leave, the conversation finished, but stopped when Jameson took a step.

"But sir," he stopped at Everett's sharp look, then forged on, voice tight and controlled. "The bayou floods; even now the waters are at the edge of the fields. The crossing will be cut off in less than an hour. The river—"

"Then the road will be cut off," Everett spat, impatient and irritable. The cotton had to be salvaged. The fortune of Rosewood now hinged, unfortunately, on the very bayou that was threatening its livelihood, the boggy waterway necessary to transport the crop to its eventual point of sale. Not a soul on the plantation, save Everett, was aware that this was the final sale, that the Blackburn's would be leaving this land in the coming months and migrating south. Cotton had ceased to be the most lucrative agricultural crop on the horizon, and Everett was nothing if not keen to be at the forefront of change. Perhaps unwisely, and uncharacteristically brazen, last month he had met with investors and sunk his net worth, and the future of Rose-wood, into a sugar plantation two hundred miles southerly.

Payment was due.

The cotton had to be sold.

"She is a strong boat. She will weather the storm." Everett schooled his face, careful not to show Jameson how the suggestion affected him. He knew the men aboard the Mary Clare, had been on the vessel many times. They were good men, hard workers, and Jameson was a fair foreman with sound judgment. If he said the dangers were too great, it was with good reason.

But the ship must launch on schedule.

Everett could read weary resignation on Jameson's face.

The foreman held Everett's cool gaze for a long moment, before nodding curtly. "Yes, sir."

The howl of the wind when Jameson pulled open the door sent a chill down Everett's spine. As a child in southern Mississippi he had witnessed an enormous storm that had turned the midday sky nearly emerald in hue, with a massive rope of cloudbank that lowered to the ground and swallowed everything in its path. Everett's home had been destroyed, but the narrow lean-to that had housed his mother's chickens and a single cow had been left standing pristine, untouched.

His mother and sister had died that day, his father not long after from his injuries.

He would never forget the sound of the wind as it converged upon the little log house, a sound he feared he now recognized roaring distant across the bayou. He quickly crossed to the door, throwing it open, the wind catching it in a fearsome draft and slamming it into the wall.

Emmeline's screams mingled with the sound of shattering glass. "Papa!"

Everett ran across the porch and down the steps, the driving rain blinding him in the black night. "Jameson!"

He spat the water that filled his mouth. "Jameson! Wait!"

He was forced to stop, the wind and rain too brutal, Emmeline's cries and the pale yellow glow of oil lamp pulling him swiftly up the steps and back into the cold marble entry. He knelt on the floor beside his daughter, soaked and shivering. He pushed her gently aside when she tried to cling, not wanting to get her nightclothes wet. "Go upstairs and get into bed, Emmeline."

"But Papa," she shook her head, jumping at a flash of lightening. The wind whistled eerily through the pierced edges of broken glass in the sidelights of the door surround.

"Now," he said firmly and Emmeline's eyes filled at his harsh tone. She ran up the steps, her bare feet padding soundlessly against the mahogany treads.

"What is it, Everett?" Father Gabriel asked from the parlor doorway. Charlotte and the serving girl Cecily stood on either side of him.

Everett forced his face into a neutral expression. "I'm afraid you will be staying with us for a bit longer than you planned, Father."

Gabriel's eyes flicked to the bits of sparkling glass on the floor, an increasing sheen of wet seeping across the marble. He nodded slowly. "Very well."

"Cecily." Charlotte pointed at the mess by the door and the servant girl hurried into the depths of the house to procure, Everett assumed, supplies.

"I think it would be best if we all retire for the evening," Everett said evenly. "This storm will blow over and the dawn will bring a new day."

He ignored the searching look the priest gave him when he turned on his heel and started up the stairs to his rooms.

Cecily's scream rent the night, a piercing wail above the hurtling sound of the wind tearing at the walls of the mansion.

Everett jumped from his bed fully clothed; some latent instinct had warned him against getting undressed for the night. Halfway down the marble stairway he stopped, staring in horror. The ground floor of the mansion was flooding, water pouring under the doorframe and through the holes punched through the sidelights. The murky water painted a deeper shade of blue along the bottom three feet of the pale silk draperies flanking the windows.

"Cecily!" He barked at the girl who stood in the center of the foyer, twisting and turning, incoherent, her bedclothes soaked. She pulled at her hair, muttering in a confused mix of French Creole and English.

He descended the remainder of the steps, sucking in a breath as the cold water soaked him to his knees. A dark flash in his peripheral vision told him Father Gabriel was on the landing. When he reached the girl he grabbed her firmly by the upper arm and dragged her back to the staircase. "Upstairs, everyone!"

The order was pointless; he and the priest were alone in the huge house with Charlotte, Emmeline and the girl who now clung limply to his side. He gestured for Gabriel to take the girl and strode quickly to Emmeline's room. The young girl was sitting in the center of her bed, rocking, tears bright in her eyes, cheeks wet. The windows rattled, walls trembling against the force of the storm, and a long, groaning reverberation spurred Everett to move quickly.

The five residents gathered in Charlotte's bedroom parlor, Emmeline on her father's lap, wrapped in a blanket to buffer the harshest of the storm's noise. When the shutters were ripped from the windows with a tearing screech, she whimpered into his neck and he held her tighter.

"The barns will not have survived this gale," Father Gabriel said softly. "You will have lost your horses."

Everett met his gaze and held it; both men knew the horses were not all that would be lost. He turned his head and focused on the expensive damask wallpaper lining the walls of the pretty little parlor and thought of the dozens of empty rooms surrounding them, safe from the hell the dark had yet to deliver.

This house, a safe harbor in a storm to end all storms.

There would be no safe harbor for the Mary Clare.

The remainder of the night was spent huddled near the fire, as the wind and the rain raged on interminably. The stench of the bayou was thick in the air and Everett knew that all possessions on the ground floor would be in ruins. Were it not for the sheer breadth and scope of

Rosewood, he was not sure the house itself might not lift from its very foundation and float down the bayou to join with the Ouachita and then on to the sea.

When the first lights of dawn broke across the eastern sky, Everett and the priest ventured quietly down the steps, Charlotte and the two younger females still sleeping. The ground floor was covered in water, but the depth had receded, perhaps two inches from its highest point as marked on the wall with a grey tinge of grime.

Everett paused at the window on the landing, a hand covering his mouth at the devastation revealed by the new day's light.

Rosewood stood majestic, an island in a sea of mud and silt and water, no other land visible, the bayou having converged with the river to turn this narrow plain of land into a new body of water.

Father Gabriel gasped and the sound startled Everett. His eyes followed the shaking tip of the man's finger to the edge of what would have formerly been the rose garden.

Face down, a body was floating.

Then another, and another.

And yet more, until all Everett could see were the bodies, bobbing in the current, swept in a gentle wave past the great, marble house, as its master absorbed from a second story window the bleak consequences of the storm.

IT TOOK twelve days for the water to recede.

Even then, Rosewood was cut off from whatever civilization remained in the aftermath of the storm. The narrow dirt and rock channel that had breached the bayou, providing the main house access to the rest of the world, had washed away. It would have to be rebuilt.

Father Gabriel, in a surprising show of fortitude, had proven to be handy both with carpenter's tools and in the kitchen, where supplies were now running dangerously low. He and Cecily had managed to stretch what meager foodstuffs they could salvage from the pantry until the root cellar was once more accessible. While it too had partially flooded, many of the vegetables inside were intact.

At dusk on the thirteenth day, Everett was interrupted in his work stacking the rotting, mildewed furnishings from the ground floor for later burning by Cecily's frantic call.

"Sir. Sir!"

Everett sighed and brushed his filthy hands on his trousers, crossing the mud-spattered floor to the doorway. Emmeline stood at Cecily's side, clutching at her skirts. Charlotte was nowhere to be seen, but that was not unusual; she had been keeping to her rooms since the storm.

"What is it?"

Cecily raised her free arm, pointing. A figure crossed the wet grounds, black cape dragging through the mud behind her, deep auburn hair piled high upon her head.

"It's Apolline," Cecily whispered, frantically making the sign of the cross.

"Don't be ridiculous," Everett muttered, squinting. "The bayou is impassible."

"Boat, mebbe," Cecily whispered brokenly, backing toward the door, taking Emmeline with her.

The woman continued in her sedate pace until she stood at the foot of the marble steps.

"Everett Blackburn." Her skin was porcelain, creamy, and her lips were blood red.

Everett felt the hair rise on the back of his neck and he resisted the urge to swipe his hand across the damp skin. "Apolline."

The witch inclined her head with a satisfied smile. "I am honored, sir."

Everett raised an eyebrow at the cordial greeting. Tales of Apolline's power and vindictiveness were known far and wide, and local chatter about the witch had carried into the big house via the fast-moving grapevine of household employees. Everett held no personal belief in her familiarity with or power over the occult, however.

"Your family will leave here this night by boat."

Everett frowned. "I would be most grateful for your assistance, Apolline, I thank you." He took one step closer to the edge of the porch, looming over the woman, drawn to her oddly colored amber eyes. "We are nearing the end of our supplies."

"You will remain." The smile was gone in a flash, along with the light in her eyes, and Everett felt a cool breeze wrap around his temple before it dipped down his spine, chilling him to the bone.

"I'm afraid I do not understand—"

"Silence!" Apolline held up a graceful palm and in the heartbeat it took for her to close it into a fist, Everett felt the air squeezed from his throat. He clutched at his neck, ripping the button free, clawing at his skin for breath.

Apolline dropped her hand and he gasped, bent over at the waist.

"The Mary Clare is at the bottom of the ocean, good sir. Your greed and avarice are responsible for the deaths of all two hundred souls aboard."

Everett could hear her voice, it rang in his ears, a quiet hum that filled his head though her lips never moved.

"You alone will repay the debt. One year for every soul." She cocked her head and smiled brightly. "Your family will go free."

"You are insane," Everett rasped, throat burning, raw. His eyes watered as a peculiar sense of displacement enveloped him.

Apolline twisted her wrist and Everett fell to his knees, crying out as pain tore through his chest.

"You are destined to remain in this house, cut off from the world you so eagerly desired to possess. One year," she stepped closer and Everett whimpered, falling, knuckles catching against the uppermost tread before he toppled end over end to the ground.

When he lay at her feet, gasping, she smiled beatifically. "One year, for every soul."

He flinched when she kneeled. She brushed a cool, soft hand against his brow and down his cheek. He would have scrambled away, but he was frozen, paralyzed.

"You are beautiful, Everett," she crooned. "I had no idea. Too beautiful, I fear, to suffer the fate I had planned. I am loathe to be so cruel." She traced his eyebrows, the bridge of his nose, pausing before touching a single fingertip to his lips. "Shhh," she whispered, and only then did he realize the soft whine in his head was coming from his throat.

She lowered her head to brush her lips softly across his, the brief flick of her tongue wetting the seam of his mouth. Her breath was warm on his chin when she spoke. "You," she kissed him again. "Are a monster."

Her lips feathered across his cheekbone until they reached his eyes and he blinked them closed in defense.

"I cannot change what I have wrought," she said sadly, rocking back on her heels. She studied him. "But I can add to your penance, my pretty Everett, with the face of an angel."

She was on her feet and the cape fluttered in the sudden updraft. "Two hundred years is your due, and this house," she gestured, the sweep of her arm encompassing the mud-tinged grounds surrounding them. "This land, your prison. But I can be a generous lover, dear angel. I grant you the gift of flight." She bowed her head and chanted, and Everett's ears filled with the sound of her voice and the drone of the wind, until he cried out, grabbing his head between his hands.

"Apolline!" Father Gabriel stood at the top of the steps, a worn bible and rosary in hand.

"Cease." Apolline flung a finger in his direction and Gabriel flew against the wall of the house, head cracking against the marble, book and beads scattering across the porch. She finished her chant and smiled down at Everett in delight. "This is your destiny, Everett. But I have made it glorious. For you will have the wings of an angel, to match your pretty face. Alas," she squinted into the fading sun. "I cannot prevent the monster from accompanying the change. But you deserve nothing less and I am comfortable with my choices. For two hundred years you will walk, or," she laughed and the sound chilled Everett to the bone. "Fly bound to these grounds. With your dutiful companion." She flicked her finger and Gabriel, too, fell to the porch.

She stepped back and Everett gulped a fresh lungful of air as the pain in his chest and the ringing in his ears subsided. He flexed his fingers but lay still, stunned, as she continued to speak.

"In the two hundredth year, a pure soul will appear. Win this heart with love and compassion and grace, despite the creature you present, and the curse will be broken. You will be free to live out the remainder of your days as a man once more."

Everett drew back when she reached for his face, finding he had regained control of his limbs. He scrabbled for purchase on the wet ground.

Apolline laughed at the futility of his movements. "Two hundred years, sir. With eternity as your punishment should you not be found worthy."

"Father," Everett gasped, when she turned to go, concerned for the priest who climbed unsteadily to his feet.

"Father Gabriel." Apolline approached the porch, smiling serenely when the priest flinched backward. "You will remain with Everett until the curse is broken. If you abandon the land that this house stands on for more than twelve hours, you will die."

"I don't believe in your curses, witch," the priest ground out between bloody lips.

"I am not a witch," Apolline inclined her head. "Time will show you the error of your logic, good sir. You are a man of faith. I trust you will be an honorable companion for our angel." She turned to leave. "Heed my warning, Father. This land will remain a lonely and forbidding specter for the people here from this day forward. The death that permeates this ground will be avenged."

Gabriel staggered down the steps in her wake to help Everett to his feet. He scraped the blood from his lip. "She is nothing more than a witch doctor, Everett, playing on the natives' fears and spreading the same as if a fungus."

Everett's eyes scanned the edge of moss-covered cypress lining the bayou's edge, but the witch had vanished. He shivered. "I am not worried."

But the words rang false and cold in the dusk.

~

Everett jerked awake, dragged from a restless slumber. He blinked into the darkness and sat up. The moon was full, and when the clouds parted a sheath of silver light poured through the window, illuminating his bed. He listened intently; perhaps Emmeline had called out, although Charlotte's rooms were closer to their daughter than his own.

He rubbed his face to shake off the last vestiges of sleep and swung his legs to the floor. His shoulder blade twitched, a nagging, biting itch, and he craned his hand behind his back, fruitlessly trying to reach it.

A sudden, excruciating pain blazed through his spine, and he cried out, falling to his hands on the bed. His shoulders, his back, his very bones were on fire and he tried to call for help, but then the skin over his scapula ruptured, releasing a jutting, mangled bone, and he collapsed on the bedcovers. Guttural, animalistic sounds were torn from his throat as his body convulsed on the bed. He bit through his lip and blood ran down his chin, the dark red dampness mirroring the wetness he could feel seeping across his back.

Another pulse of pain so hot and bright it eclipsed all thought threw him to the floor and he clawed at the hooked rug, watching in shock as his silhouette was outlined in sprays of fresh blood. His back exploded with a foreign sensation, heavy, hard, as something unnatural draped and dragged across his skin. It unfurled and fell to the rug with a sticky splat of congealed blood and tissue. He retched, spitting bile, coughing, tears leaking from his eyes when a new pain emerged, this time in his feet.

He could only shudder limply against the bed frame when the bedroom door was flung open.

"Oh holy Father, what have you done?" Father Gabriel cried.

Everett lifted one shaking, trembling hand toward the door, in a silent plea for help as blackness sank in around him. The last sounds he heard were Charlotte's hysterical screams.

CHAPTER 1

$\mathcal{N}$oah Hix was not a fan of flying.

If he *were* a fan of flying, he wouldn't be stuck on the side of a cracked and broken two-lane blacktop in backwater Louisiana trying in vain to find the *fucking* highway on the tiny maze of lines on this *fucking* useless map.

He shoved the thick paper aside, barely containing the urge to crumple it into a tight ball, and flicked the wipers as high as they would go, wands slicking across the thick swath of rain that pounded the windshield. Visibility was nil, the downpour now obliterating the road in the darkness. He eased off the brake and gently pushed the accelerator, maneuvering the car into what he hoped was his lane, although he suspected if it wasn't, he wouldn't know until it was too late to course correct.

The 1969 Plymouth Road Runner might be a gorgeous classic, but nimble she was not.

He hit a pothole and winced as the big blue car bounced across the wet pavement, leather-wrapped steering wheel jerking hard under his hands.

"Dark and stormy nights my ass," he muttered. His brother George had called just before the storm's force hit him for real, feeding him the cheesy line and telling him to be careful as he crisscrossed the back country. Noah had taken the advice to heart, avoiding interstates clogged with residents and vacationers alike, all fleeing the unrelenting trek of hurricane Idabell.

George had escaped on one of the last flights out of Louis Armstrong International, along with their childhood friend Maxie, and they had probably landed in Kansas City by now. Both had insisted that Noah go with them; as if Noah would ever leave his most prized possession behind. He had spent far too many hours and far too much money restoring the classic car to risk losing her now.

It was one of the only things he and his dad had ever agreed upon.

George and Maxie would have ridden back with him, had Max not fallen inexplicably and disgustingly ill the day prior to the hurricane's ugly turn toward the Louisiana shoreline. They had purchased two plane tickets mere hours before the weather channel first breathed the word *evacuation*. Noah had convinced them to keep their reservation; after all, he had been fine returning to Kansas City alone before the impending storm, why would a little rain and wind change that now?

It had been quite a week. The three friends had driven down to New Orleans on a lark, Noah missing the days when he and George would jump in the car and ramble across the Kansas prairie in search of adventure, and Max needing an escape from the constant threat of slowly turning into her mother. And it had been more fun than Noah had had in months. Good food, good beer, good company.

A flash of lightning interrupted Noah's musings and suddenly there was a tree lying across the previously barren road.

Noah slammed on the brakes, tires catching on the wet, slick road and locking, skidding, the backend fishtailing as the heavy piece of machinery tried to flip around. He spun to a stop with maybe a foot to spare, chest tight with a lungful of air. He released it in a rush, sweat popping on his forehead, fingers clenched on the steering wheel.

"Fuck," he exhaled shakily. Tentatively, he nudged the car into gear again and sighed in relief when the tires caught pavement. "Stupid, stupid, stupid," he chanted, carefully negotiating the narrow road, forward and reverse, until he was moving against the rain, in the direction from which he'd just come. There had been an opening back there in the dark, and he hoped it was marked on that goddamn map, because it looked like that little road was his last hope against the storm.

~

"THE STORM IS KICKING UP. Idabell, they're calling it." Gabriel passed Everett a glass of iced tea, the square cubes clinking against the clear mug.

Everett grunted. "Nostalgic name," he muttered, grimacing at the bland bitterness of the tea. "Are we out of sugar, then?"

Gabriel rolled his eyes and produced two small pink packets. "Use these, it's all we've got until I can go into town for supplies." Everett's carefully schooled expression, and failure to move to take the sweetener, had Gabriel squirming on the settee. "Don't look at me like that."

"I refuse to consume that ridiculous, unnatural concoction." Everett sniffed primly, dispelling the impending gloom that had settled over Gabriel.

Everett was disgruntled and melancholy at the best of times; Gabriel had learned long ago to read his moods and find shelter from the tempest when it was bad. And as the years progressed, it had often been bad.

It had been the motive for building a small cabin behind the house, Gabriel's refuge, and source of self-preservation, although the structure had taken he and Rett nearly a year to construct, and almost another to fully wire and plumb. Construction, Gabriel was familiar with, having raised many a barn and roof in his days as a traveling priest. The other trade skills he had had to learn, but, in two hundred years he had had little else on his hands but time. And a conveniently located library in the tiny town of Revelation just down the bayou.

Convincing the parish utility providers to venture behind the cypress-lined waterways to the old (and oft-rumored haunted) Rosewood plantation to install services hadn't been without its share of troublesome coercion. The payoff, however, was grand. Gabriel had a small television, and after a well was dropped on the backside of the property, hot and cold running water. His tiny kitchen held a refrigerator and stove and microwave. But his most favorite invention of the past two hundred years was in the living space: a window air conditioning unit.

Sometimes, on the steamiest summer nights, he would lie naked in the center of his bed, blissful in the cool blast of air as it evaporated the film of sweat that seemed ever present on his skin in this godforsaken swamp.

Everett still refused air conditioning, (Gabriel attributed this stubbornness to his annoying habit of martyrdom) but the miracle of heated water had convinced him to allow Gabriel to wire the central living space of Rosewood as well. The right and left wings of the mansion remained much as they had been in the 19th century.

Television was not an allowable luxury either.

Nothing was going to be a luxury if Rett didn't allow him to sell another piece of art or antiquity soon.

"Rett—"

A loud burst of thunder shook the window glass and the lights flickered before they were thrust into darkness.

Everett unerringly placed his glass on the small table beside his chair with a soft *clink*.

Gabriel, blind in the newly blackened room, frowned when he felt more than saw Everett move past him. "Where are you going?" He stared into the nothing, trying to discern shapes, shadows.

"To bed."

A flash of lightning pushed an elongated shadow of Rett' form against the opposite wall as he climbed the staircase. Gabriel blinked rapidly, the afterimage of wings burnt onto his eyelids. Somewhere overhead a door closed with a muted thud.

"And you have a good evening, too," he murmured, snorting. He stood and held out his hands, carefully making his way across the room and managing to reach the doorway without banging a shin or stubbing a toe. Another harsh bolt of too-close atmospherical charge afforded him a cursory view of the rest of his path through the kitchen, where he could find his way by feel, if not by sight, to the back door.

From there, he had only to make it across the yard to his little cabin hideaway to ride out the storm.

CHAPTER 2

The road was a dead end.

It was paved, until the decaying blacktop gave way to densely packed dirt and ended abruptly in a muddy two-tire trail at a line of trees. The smell of what Noah quickly learned was swamp water filled the car when he cracked his window. He sat for a long moment, staring at the thick, grey moss hanging in eerie drapes from the cypress that edged what he suspected was a body of moving water. He could hear the rush under the pounding rain.

He put the car in reverse, not trusting the sodden ground not to swallow the car's wheels if he tried to turn her around. "Fuck this fucking state and its fucking stinky water hellhole of a road system," he cursed under his breath as he navigated the trail backwards, head craned around.

He had to stop when his neck cramped and he pounded the steering wheel in frustration. He was seriously contemplating sleeping through Idabell, right there on the front seat, when a light between the trees startled him. He blinked, thinking it was a hallucination, or the car's headlamps reflecting off a distant spot of dampness.

The light moved.

It was small and round and glowing, and it flickered through the cypress and the moss, dancing and blinking out of existence only to reappear a second later. It climbed in altitude, slowly, further away, then near, higher and higher until it was gone for so long Noah was sure he had imagined it.

When it winked back into view, constant and stationary, he realized it was a flashlight; no, a candle. The light was too warm and yellow to be artificial.

"Finally," he exhaled and backed up, excruciatingly slow, eyes scanning the trees for an opening. When he spotted it, he grinned. "Hallelujah."

His smile faded as he descended an overgrown set of tire tracks, halting at the perimeter of a very intimidating crossing. He wouldn't dare call that thing a bridge; it was a pile of rocks that looked like it had been gathered by a beaver for a dam, and Noah had serious doubts as to whether it would withstand the weight of the car. Especially with him *in* it. He was half-tempted to reverse and continue back out to the highway when the light beyond the trees began to move again. He could see a window clearly now, tall and narrow, old-fashioned, and the outline of the house it belonged to in the next strike of lightning made his mouth go dry.

"Holy shit."

The choice was made for him when the car began to slide in the damp and mud, and it was either hit the gas and cross the bayou or sink into the water that trickled across the top of the crossing in a thin sheen.

Noah hit the gas.

There was no drive, per se, once he made it safely across the water, but he could see the hood of a vintage Ford pickup peeking around the end of one wing. It would have born further investigating, were the weather not potentially about to become disastrous, and Noah not fighting a surprisingly strong desire to flee.

There was something foreboding about this house.

It was enormous, and dark, although he could appreciate that at one point it had been a beauty. Greek in style, the portico was massive, topped with a triangular pediment and flanked on all sides by fluted columns. The centerpiece was easily three stories, and probably included a spooky attic (if Noah's experiences with old houses held), and there were identical two-story wings on either side. A house this size, tucked into the backwoods of nowhere Louisiana, had been here a while.

A good, long while.

Noah shivered as he stood in front of the massive door. The rain and wind had beat against his back as he made a run for the steps, and now the moisture that had gathered under his collar ran down his spine. He searched in vain for a doorbell before giving up and lifting the ornate brass knocker. It fell with a dull *thud,* the sound carrying even over the torrent of water that fell from the sky.

Then, he waited.

∾

TWIN ARCS of light flooded Gabriel's little house and he jumped out of bed.

"Holy God," he breathed in shock. He stared as the lights of what was obviously a car climbed the sloping yard before halting in front of the main house. He yanked on his pants and boots and grabbed a flashlight before racing to the backdoor of the main house.

With the exception of the (exorbitantly bribed) drilling company and electric coop, not a single soul had voluntarily ventured onto Rosewood plantation in two hundred years.

Gabriel's heart hammered in his chest with the implication.

∾

NOAH DROPPED THE KNOCKER AGAIN. "Come on," he muttered, flipping the collar of his jacket up to buffer his neck against the wind. He banged a fist against the door. "Hello?"

He backed up, peering in the area where he had seen the candle. A soft yellow-red glow cast an oddly-shaped shadow in the narrow rectangular opening and he waved; someone up there was watching him. "Yeah, I'm down here, douchebag. Now come open the door."

The window went dark.

~

GABRIEL CAREENED UP THE STAIRS, skidding to a stop on the first landing when the car's driver began to bang on the door. He peered out the window but couldn't see the man. He took the rest of the steps as quietly as he could, bursting into Everett's bedroom.

"Rett—"

"I've seen him. Get rid of him."

Everett's back was to the door as he stared out into the darkness. Rain peppered the window, and from the glow of his downturned flashlight, Gabriel could just make out his scowl, water droplets sparkling like jewels against the firm jaw of his reflection. Great, dark wings dragged the floor behind him, his presence in the shadowed room larger than his body alone would suggest. When Gabriel didn't move to leave, Everett tensed and the musculature under the skin of his back rippled in response, reminding Gabriel of just how much the outwardly cool exterior hid. Everett had learned well to control his rage over the long span of suspended time, but even a gentle beast, when cornered, will attack.

"The storm. Don't you think we should," Gabriel stopped. Any storm was a touchy subject, and one he knew better than to approach.

"Get rid of him," Rett warned, voice rough, scraping low and dangerous along Gabriel's spine.

Even after all these shared years, the former priest was still mindful of the careful negotiations required of his station in this mixed up tale that once had been his life.

And yet.

"He could be the one." Gabriel let the words settle over both of them, quiet.

Calm.

The old house was filled with the silence of a structure undertaking a deluge; rain slaking across the thick panes of glass, lightning shattering the bleak darkness in carefully measured increments behind each thunderous crack of heaven splitting open. The foundation creaked and the roof joints whined.

All things had a breaking point, Gabriel knew. Even those exceptionally well crafted and thoughtfully, even maliciously, planned.

"Don't be ridiculous," Everett finally said.

"Rett—"

"No!" Everett's roar was mutinous, abrupt and cold, and it shook the frame of the window where he stood, as surely as any thunder had before. The sleek expanse of his wings threw a deep shadow across the wall in the flashlight's weak illumination.

His claws clicked on the floor as he shifted position, nostrils flaring, feathered appendages lowering in remorse, perhaps even shame, but Gabriel kept his eyes trained on Everett's profile.

"Is it to be you and I then?" he asked, voice barely above a whisper as he backed toward the door. "Forever, old friend?"

Everett hung his head tiredly and turned back to the dark night outside the window, staring down at the twin triangular domes of light spraying across the overgrowth along the front path. He didn't answer.

He couldn't, there were no more words. Because after all these many decades, with time effectively running out, Everett had long since lost all hope.

He didn't move for several moments after the door clicked closed behind him.

GABRIEL TOOK a deep breath and pulled the heavy door open.

The porch's occupant whirled around in surprise, a grin lighting his handsome face.

"Thank God, I thought you were going to leave me out here to drown."

Gabriel winced inwardly. "I cannot help you, you should go." He started to close the door and the man's hand shot out, quick, to stop him.

"Wait. I just need some help getting back to the highway, and," the man grinned tentatively again, coughing. "Maybe I could use your facilities?"

Gabriel stared at him in silence for so long the man shifted his weight back and forth.

"Look, man, I'm lost. And in case you hadn't noticed," he waved a finger in the air over his head. "We're in the middle of a goddamned hurricane."

"I can't help you." Gabriel put all of his weight behind his next shove and the door closed resolutely in the man's stunned face. Gabriel's forehead made a soft thud when it hit the cool wood. "Father, forgive me," he whispered, wondering if they had sealed this man's fate as surely as the fates of two hundred others so many years ago.

Noah stared at the door in shock. "Sonofa—"

He kicked the door in frustration. "Thanks a lot, asshole!" he yelled and kicked the door once more for good measure. He turned back to the rain and the dark and, resolute, descended the steps at a jog, sliding into the warm mugginess of the car. "Sonofabitch," he repeated. He glanced at the map, but ignored it, choosing instead to favor raw instinct. And common sense.

He had turned right. So he would retrace his steps and turn left.

He eased down the makeshift drive, sucking in a breath at what awaited him at the crossing. Water now flowed freely over it, the mud and rock surface murky under the glow of his headlights. He gritted his teeth and nudged the gas.

He was halfway across, heaving a sigh of relief, when a wall of water, fed by the swollen river and gaining strength by the second, flung an errant tree limb under the Road Runner and pushed her over the side.

"Fuck!" Noah swore, hitting the gas and jerking the steering wheel, desperately attempting to right the car before she fell into the bayou. The car stalled, teetering on the edge, the back end hung up, wheels spinning fruitlessly. When the water began to stream into the floorboard, Noah knew he had to bail.

"Fuck fuck fuck," he hissed, rolling down the driver's window and gauging his chances. The water was violent as it rushed under him, and the tipsy shuddering of the car made his stomach dip in fear; if his weight proved too much as he jumped into the bayou, the car could flip over on top of him. "Passenger side it is," he muttered and unlatched his seatbelt.

He climbed carefully over the middle seat and removed the keys from the ignition; God willing, when the water receded he could walk out here and start 'er up, drive on home.

"Yeah right," he complained under his breath, climbing out of the passenger door. The river-heavy bayou was cold and instantly filled his boots. The ground of the crossing felt unsteady, disintegrating under the combined weight of the car and the water, and Noah knew instinctively he needed to hurry. He shut the door with as little force as possible and held onto the shining black body as he picked his way across the eddying flow. He patted the trunk sadly. "I'll be back for you, sweetheart, don't you worry."

He never saw the second tree limb as it swept over the side of the crossing and knocked him into the deep.

CHOKING. Dark, cold and wet.

Noah gasped when his head broke the surface, wheezing, coughing, swallowing another mouthful of filth before retching and being dragged beneath, the undertow too swift, the bottom too far away. He kicked furiously, jeans weighting his legs, boots leaden, sinking, the darkness of the night and the storm disorienting him. He swam, arms straining, lungs burning with the need to express the liquid he had inhaled, and he kicked harder, but he had no idea if he was pushing himself deeper to the bottom or closer to the top.

Far too soon he felt his arms weaken, and his legs lighten. A strange sense of euphoria swept through him and he wondered if he had kicked free, was saved, if he was even now gasping fresh, clean mouthfuls of air, lying on the moss-covered ground under an ancient cypress. *Georgie,* he thought. *I'm coming home.*

He felt, rather than saw the darkness deepen, encompassing him, clutching him within its confines and wrapping him in a cocoon of warmth, lifting him free of the wetness and the cold emptiness of dying alone, and he clung to it.

With his last whisper of consciousness he projected, *thank you,* and hoped there was someone on the other side to receive him.

Gabriel scrambled to get out the way when his front door slammed into the wall, screaming wind and torrential rain heralding Everett's appearance in the opening. The winged creature crossed the room in three strides before unceremoniously dropping the unconscious man he held over his shoulder onto Gabriel's bed.

"What have you done?" Gabriel rushed to the bedside, peeling back one of the man's eyelids, laying his ear to the man's chest. He shivered when he heard the swift flutter of feathers and felt a spray of water on his back.

"He was in the bayou."

Gabriel held his breath, listening hard.

"Is he—"

"Shh," Gabriel shushed him, repositioning his ear. His hand scraped under the man's jaw and along his throat, searching for the pulse of life he knew should flicker there. He held his breath, tuning out the sound of the storm and the drip drip drip of the moisture that slipped from Rett' wings and pinged against the hardwood. The skin under his fingers was cool but there was a hint of warmth beneath and maybe—

He breathed a sigh of relief when he felt it, a thready *bump-bump* under the pad of his middle finger, and *there,* beneath the soaked plaid cotton shirt, the beat of his heart. "He's alive," he exhaled shakily. "He's alive."

As if on cue the man moaned, before folding in on himself with a wracking cough, retching filthy bile and water all over the bed.

Gabriel grimaced, holding the man firmly on his side until he was still. "Fetch me some towels, Everett, and clean linens."

Everett grumbled under his breath, obviously anxious to make his escape, but he dutifully left to retrieve the items from the bathroom. Gabriel winced when he heard the tinkling sound of shattering glass as an errant wing knocked something loose.

This was a house meant for man, not beast.

He peered down at the stranger who remained unconscious after releasing the contents of his stomach and lungs. He was pale, too pale, in the light from the oil lamp, and a quick palm against his forehead confirmed that he was clammy and trembling as well. Gabriel quickly unbuttoned the flannel shirt; the man was going into shock.

"Rett!"

"Here." Everett tossed the towels across the room, most of them falling within Gabriel's reach, as he remained poised for flight, statue-still by the bathroom door.

Gabriel spread open the man's shirt and grabbed the nearest towel, vigorously rubbing the moisture from his chest, urging a sluggish bloodstream to the surface. He glanced at the room's only other occupant. "Are you going to stand over there brooding or are you going to help?"

"He could awaken at any moment. I should go."

"Take off his boots, and his jeans," Gabe said, ignoring him. "He's chilled. We need to remove his wet things and warm him."

Everett opened his mouth to protest but slammed it shut at Gabriel's warning glare. "Fine." He shook his wings again, the remaining water sluicing off and spattering the walls and furnishings.

"And could you please stop doing that?" Gabe groused under his breath, startling when Everett appeared at his side in an instant. "Sorry," he muttered.

"You care too much for material possessions, Father." Everett grabbed one of the man's boots and deftly untied the strings, pulling it free and tossing it to the floor by the door. He repeated the motion with the second boot then hesitated, unsure.

"I'm no longer a priest, as you are aware," Gabriel said calmly, pulling the man's arm free and sliding the shirt out from under him. He glanced pointedly at the man's jeans. "Pants."

"I—" Everett stopped, flustered. He growled low in his throat to mask his frustration and shifted closer to the bed. His fingers worked the buttons on the fly open before tugging the pants down the man's hips. They clung to his skin, sodden and heavy, and Everett's fingers tingled when they brushed the clamminess underneath. He grunted again as he worked the pants lower, blinking when they suddenly slipped free to the man's thighs, dragging his undergarment with them.

Gabriel chuckled at Rett' expression and tossed a dry towel over the man's groin. "Don't look so stunned, Rett. I'm pretty sure you were already aware he was male."

"Shut up," Rett warned, recovering his composure to yank the man's pants down his calves and tossing them to the floor.

Gabriel stood. "Pick him up."

"What? Why?" Rett backed up two steps. He tried desperately to look anywhere but at the naked man lying on Gabriel's bed and failed miserably. The cut of his jaw was beautiful in the lamplight, and even at this distance, Everett could see freckles dusting over his cheekbones and the bridge of his nose. His upper body was broad and showed evidence the man was a laborer, waist pleasingly narrow in contrast, and his skin was an appealing deep gold, work worn and oft exposed to the sun. The pale cream of his bare hips were a sharp contrast in the low light of the room, and Everett's fingertips tingled again in latent memory of their soft smoothness.

He had touched no one, nor been touched, in two centuries.

"No."

"Rett." Gabriel sighed and shoved the clean linens in Rett' direction. "Fine. I'll lift him and you—"

Rett pushed him aside before he could finish and easily lifted the man in his arms. He turned away so that Gabriel had room to strip the bed, one wing lifting to allow his friend to pass under it.

The man's head hung limply over the crook of his elbow, exposing a long column of throat. Rett could see the pulse fluttering rapidly just under his jaw, but he didn't need the visual confirmation that the man was alive; he could hear his heartbeat, could feel the blood pumping through his veins.

It was heady. And frighteningly unusual.

Everett's blood responded in kind, pricking to life with a hum. His forearms burned where they touched the man's naked skin, and he felt a sudden, intense urge to fly. "Finish it," he ground out between his teeth.

"Fine, fine," Gabriel soothed. "It's finished." He held up the sheet and motioned for Rett to deposit the man under it.

For all that he wanted to drop the man and flee into the storm, wash away the strange feeling snaking through his limbs, Rett was gentle as he arranged him on the bed. He pulled the towel free from the man's hips as Gabriel lowered the sheet.

"I'll probably—" Gabriel blinked. Rett was already gone, shoving past him and out, into the rain and wind and dark.

Noah was first aware of a sharp ache in his neck and back, as if all his joints and sockets had been wrenched by opposing forces, his body tossed about in abandon. His arms were heavy, eyelids weighted. He fought the cottony, warm sleep that wanted to contain him in its depths, holding him tight, promising peaceful slumber, safety from the cold and the wet and the—

His eyes popped open as the memory washed over him, water, rain, the bayou filling his lungs. He gasped, chest expanding painfully, inducing a coughing fit that forced him onto his side in an attempt to relieve the aching pressure. It felt like his lungs had been wrung inside out and then shoved back down his throat. His breath rattled, wet and unsteady, and he glanced blearily at his sparse surroundings, memories of the storm and becoming lost in the bayou flooding back.

From this vantage point, he appeared to be alone. He tentatively raised one arm above the sheet and fought to leverage himself into a sitting position. The room swam and he froze until the walls stopped spinning. *So, no sudden movements,* he thought wryly. He blinked sleepily and raked his palm across dry, chapped lips. His mouth and tongue were tacky, gross. He needed a drink, and he grimaced, disbelieving his body's craving for *water* of all things.

He cleared his dry throat and tried to call out, but his rasping *hello,* was a rustle of unintelligible syllables.

He started when the door opened and a man stepped into the small room, humming, a basket over his arm.

"Oh," the man said, immobilized by the sight of Noah staring back at him. "You're awake."

"Where," Noah tried to speak and had to swallow, his voice cracking on the single word, throat on fire from the effort. "What happened?" he tried again.

The man carefully set the basket on the floor and closed the door. Noah could see tan and cream eggs inside the small, woven container. "There was a storm," the man began hesitantly. He moved to the end of the bed and sat gingerly on the edge of the mattress. "You were swept into the bayou."

"I remember," Noah nodded, grimacing and holding his throat. "Water."

"Oh," the man shot up. "Of course. You must be parched."

He disappeared through a small doorway and Noah could hear the rattle of glassware and a faucet. He returned with a mug and held it to Noah's lips. His hands were shaking and Noah cupped one hand around the glass to steady it before drinking greedily, coughing when the burn from swallowing became too strong.

"Easy," the man murmured. "You gave us, me, quite a fright."

"Where am I?" Noah asked, falling back against the hard mattress, the simple act of taking a drink having exhausted him. He clutched at the sheet. "I," he paused, memory banks searching for something, anything after the moment he climbed from the car and onto the crossing. There was nothing. Dark, cold water. Then warmth and a breeze, weightless, and—

"Louisiana," the man offered hesitantly and Noah snorted back a laugh.

"I remember that part," he managed around a groan as he pushed himself back off the bed. He peered under the sheet. "I remember having clothes too."

The man gestured through the doorway where he had procured the cup. "They're hanging to dry, in the sun. You were," he bit his lip. "You were soaked, and very, very lucky."

"How'd you find me? I seem to remember you not being particularly happy to see me on your porch." Noah studied the man's reaction to his acknowledgement that he recognized him. He sat up straight. "My car."

"I pulled it out this morning. I'm not sure it will run, but it's free of the swamp." He held out a hand. "Gabriel."

Noah clasped the warm, dry fingers in his own, noting the firmness of the handshake, the sincerity strange and intriguing when paired with the odd note of trepidation he could see in the man's eyes. "Noah Hix."

Gabriel stood up. "I'll check on your clothes, Mr. Hix. And then we'll see about some food. Do you feel as though you could eat?"

"Noah." Noah refused the hand when he tried to stand, awkwardly wrapping the sheet around his waist. He swayed unsteadily for a moment until his equilibrium stabilized and he was able to take a step on his own. "Bathroom?" he asked, nodding toward the far door.

"Yes, of course. I'll be right back."

Noah watched the odd little man hurry from the room. He seemed torn between an eagerness to help and a fearful anxiety that Noah couldn't quite get a read on. He groaned as he limped across the smooth hardwood floor toward the bathroom, giving the cheery rag rugs and simple furnishings a cursory glance.

He relieved himself, thankful when he found modern plumbing. The simple cabin had the air of something from a bygone era, no modern amenities or frivolities immediately apparent. He washed his face and arms in the narrow pedestal sink, somewhat surprised to find the water plentiful and hot. The soap was a crudely cut bar, clearly homemade, and he brought it to his nose and gave it a sniff. It was homey and reminded him of something way back in the depths of his memory wells. Something from when he was very small, but it flitted away before he could grasp it. He laid the bar back on the plain porcelain saucer and left the bathroom.

The walls of the combination living and sleeping area were hewn log, but the double hung windows appeared new, the glass clean and sparkling in the bright morning sun. He leaned over to peer out into the front yard, surprised to find himself staring at what appeared to be a wing of the mansion from the night before.

"Are you all right?"

Noah started, grabbing the sheet before it fell and inadvertently gave his host an eyeful. "Ah, yeah. Better, thanks." He shifted uncomfortable. "Clothes?"

"Your, um," Gabriel held out Noah's boxers and Noah took them, along with his shirt. "Your pants are still very damp. I can get them, if you think," he trailed off, unsure.

Noah tilted his head in the direction of the bathroom. "If you don't mind me eating in my skivvies, I don't," he grinned.

"No, no, of course not."

Noah stepped behind the narrow door, more as a courtesy than from any modesty on his part. He had never considered himself particularly shy, about his body or anyone else's.

Gabriel wiped his hands hastily on his pants as he waited for Noah to return. "Eggs all right?"

"Eggs would be perfect," Noah called from the bathroom. "Do you have any coffee?"

"Yes, of course." Gabriel winced when a wide shadow passed over the yard. *Everett.* "I'll go start it right now," he called, voice a touch too loud. He hurried through the kitchen, forgetting to catch the back screen door before it slammed. He waved his arms frantically to the sky in warning.

Noah studied his reflection in the mirror as he buttoned the shirt. He had a shallow cut above his left eyebrow, crisscrossing a pale scar running parallel to his hairline in a jagged, twisting line. His left ear was ringing, an impossible phantom tone that had chased him for years, since he had returned from the desert battered and broken, but miraculously alive. He shook his head and snapped his fingers hard at his left temple, an old habit, and a fruitless one.

Nothing.

It was likely the water sloshing around in there, probably had already given him an infection. He sighed. That was all he needed. He had a sneaking suspicion that coffee and eggs were a lot easier to procure than antibiotics in this strange place he'd wandered into.

He ventured through the living area, feeling somewhat silly in boxers and a half-buttoned flannel shirt, feet bare on the smooth wood floor. He wondered where the man, Gabriel, had slept the night before; the furnishings were meager, spare.

He remembered his car and whirled around, peering out the front window again, but there was no sign of her. "Gabriel?" he called, but no answer came from the kitchen, so he left through the front door. He just needed to see her, know she was all right.

He was barely out from under the porch eave when the sun's light was doused, and he glanced up, praying it wasn't more rain.

The bird's wings were massive as it soared across the sky, obliterating the sun, and Noah barely resisted the urge to duck back under the porch, mouth gone slack at the size of the animal. He blinked rapidly when the sun flared bright as he tracked its flight, the wingspan forced into harsh silhouette. He rubbed his eyes but the afterimage stayed long after the shadow had passed behind the big house.

"Noah?" Gabriel asked from the doorway. "Are you all right?"

Noah heard the note of apprehension in his voice and filed it away. "Yeah, sorry." He schooled his expression before he turned and offered a bland grin. "That was a big bird."

"Carrion," Gabriel said quickly. "There were probably many animal casualties in the flood last night." He shuddered. "Hideous, disgusting birds."

Noah chuckled and ducked through the door Gabriel held open. "Not a fan of things with wings, then?" He winked at the flustered man. "Me either. Flying's overrated."

"Your coffee's ready," Gabriel blurted. At Noah's raised eyebrow he took a deep breath and released it slowly before he offered a genuine smile. "Your coffee's ready," he said again, more calmly.

Noah laughed and patted him on the arm. "Calm down, padre. I don't bite." He winked and crossed the room.

"What did you call me?" Gabriel asked, fidgeting nervously again in the kitchen doorway as he watched Noah fill two mugs.

"Padre? It's just an expression." Noah took a careful sip from one of the mugs and grunted in approval. He turned and leaned against the narrow counter, crossing one bare ankle over another. He held out the second mug.

Gabriel stepped close enough to take it and stared into the dark liquid as it lapped at the cup's white edge. "I was a priest, once," he said quietly before bringing the mug to his lips.

"No shit?" Noah cocked his head. That would explain the austerity. "What happened?" He took another sip.

"Time," Gabriel offered with a sad smile.

The pair was quiet as they drank their coffee.

"So, eggs?" Gabriel finally asked, setting the mug aside.

"How about an egg sandwich? You got any bread?" Noah grinned. "I'm guessing it's close to lunchtime by now."

"I do. And it is." Gabriel felt the tension drain from his shoulders. Noah was a happy presence, a bright and unexpected spark of life in this dreary, monotonous existence. He waved Noah aside. "If you want to go check your pants? Moisture evaporates quickly in the sun."

"Yeah, but it's so damn humid," Noah complained as he straightened. He disappeared out the back and returned a few moments later, stomach rumbling at the aroma of frying eggs and bacon. "Bacon? Padre, you're the man."

"Pants?"

"No dice," Noah said cheerfully. "I guess I'll be roaming around in my shorts for a while longer." He sat at the table and smiled his thanks when Gabriel set a plate in front of him. He frowned when the man didn't sit down across from him. "Aren't you going to eat?"

Gabriel hesitated before bringing a second plate to the table. "I didn't want to make you uncomfortable."

Noah laughed. "I'm the one in my underwear. Sit. Eat." He thumped the table with his fist. "You saved my life. I think we can break bread together."

Gabriel sat with a grin. "I accept your generous offer, Mr. Hix."

"Man, you gotta lighten up. And it's Noah."

"Noah."

They ate in companionable silence, Gabriel assembling two more sandwiches and two glasses of iced tea before they were finished.

"Ok, pants or not, I'm gonna go check on my car. You didn't happen to find my keys when you were fishing me out of the swamp, did you?"

Gabriel stood and walked to the back door, pulling Noah's car keys, cell phone and wallet from a small bowl on the counter.

"Holy shit," Noah exclaimed with a smile. "Finding one of those was probably a miracle, but all three?" He accepted the items and stood, clapping his hand to Gabriel's shoulder. "Thank you."

"You're welcome," Gabriel nodded solemnly. "Your car is just around the front of the big house."

Noah felt a little silly pulling on his boots in light of the fact that he still wasn't wearing any pants, but he didn't want to risk stepping on something disgusting in the overgrown wet yard either. He had a feeling snakes might be an issue in swampland. He could hear Gabriel cleaning up as he stepped off the porch.

He rounded the corner of the *big house*, as Gabriel had called it, and stopped to admire the pickup parked at the corner. The body was starting to show a little rust in places, but the inside looked clean and neatly kept, and Noah whistled in appreciation as he ran a hand over her rounded hood. He had grown up tinkering with cars at his Uncle Dave's shop, and after he had left the service (not entirely of his own volition), tinkering had turned into paid employment.

At the time, he had needed the familiar smells and sounds and feel of the garage to calm his shattered nerves. He didn't need both ears fully functioning to fix a motor, and the cars didn't give a shit about the ugly scars that ran across his temple or down his back.

He genuinely *liked* working for Dave, maybe even loved it. Loved reworking a motor or renovating a classic. But the pay sucked and the hours were long and sometimes he wondered if he wouldn't have done better by himself if he had gone into diesel mechanics or welding or aeronautics.

Something with a future.

The Road Runner was parked just where Gabriel had said, her hood covered in a thin film of dried muck. Noah heaved a sigh of relief when it appeared she didn't have any major cosmetic defects on his first cursory appraisal. She must not have fallen into the bayou after all. He opened the driver's door, grimacing at the stench of the overheated interior, a puddle of brackish water still present in the floorboard.

"Well you're going to be a real joy to ride home with, old girl. You stink." He slid behind the wheel and stuck the key in the ignition. "Here goes nothin'," he muttered.

The engine whined but didn't turn over and Noah pumped the gas. "Come on, baby, you can do it." He gave up when the whir of the straining motor indicated something more serious than a little too much rain.

"Fuck." He climbed back out, grabbing the cell phone and praying for a charge. He held the power button for several seconds, but the small black rectangle remained dark. "Fucking fuck," he said again, tossing the phone into the back seat.

He popped the hood and cracked his knuckles. Might as well start from the top.

"He's all right?"

"Goddammit, Rett," Gabriel jumped, dropping a plate into the sink with a clatter. "What are you doing?" he asked in a rush, glancing quickly to the front of the house. "He's right outside."

"He's at his car," Rett said smoothly. He backed off the stoop and into the shadows of the house. "He will be all right?" he asked again.

"Yes, as far as I can tell, no lasting damage. He's," he stopped and tilted his head thoughtfully, a slow grin blooming. "Seems like a nice fellow who took a wrong turn." He turned to make a crack about destiny and fate, but Everett was gone. "I really hate when you do that," he muttered, turning back to the dishes.

Noah whistled a slightly off key tune as he methodically worked through a mental checklist under the hood, wishing he could afford enough battery to hunt for a local station on the radio. And jeans. It was hot and muggy, but he was starting to feel a little weird about standing around in his boxers. The back of his neck pricked with awareness, instincts honed by years spent in a warzone, and he had turned to look behind him more times than he could count but nothing was ever there.

Just the ever-present sensation of eyes on his skin.

The clouds had gathered again, throwing the previously sunny day into an overcast gloom, and he sang aloud to dispel the distraction of the heavy atmosphere as he worked. *"And I can remember the fourth of July, runnin' through the backwood, bare. And I can still hear my old hound dog barkin', chasin' down a hoodoo there."*

He whistled the guitar riff, a song about the bayou, bent low under the hood, peering closely at a hose coupling. Something loose, maybe. He chewed his bottom lip, contemplating the muddy ground before shrugging and squatting, peering under the front end, behind the axel, looking for damage, wondering how the hell he was going to get out of this oppressive shithole.

His left side buffered by the absence of sound, Noah never heard the slick swish of the alligator as it raced across the damp grass and mud. It honed in on the warm body kneeling on the spongy earth, reptilian eyes flickering, hungry.

Noah sensed something falling over him before he saw it, a massive shadow covering the ground, and he fell to his butt in a startled attempt at evasion, frantically clawing at the grass and mud like a crab skittering across sand as *it* dropped five feet from the Road Runner's hood. He scrambled to his feet with a guttural yell, mouth working, hands grasping futilely at the slick sides of the car for traction, desperate to escape the great, hulking, *thing* he could not process, yanking open the driver's door just as the creature released a roar. The hair stood up on Noah's arms and he froze, hands on the wheel of his incapacitated car, as he spotted motion in the tall weeds of the unkempt yard, a mottled brown movement in the grasses drawing his eyes from the enormous black wings.

The alligator snapped, ferociously swinging it's powerful tail in a breathtaking standoff. Noah's lungs burned from lack of oxygen in the interminable moment it took for the gator to recoil, slinking back to the bayou and disappearing in the rushes.

His hands began to shake when the creature's wings lowered. The sun winked out from behind a cloud to cast a ray of diffused light across the yard, illuminating him from behind as he slowly turned to face the car.

He.

Because, even though Noah's brain was having trouble resolving the impossibility of what he was seeing, the thing standing before him was a man.

CHAPTER 4

"*R*ett!" Gabriel shouted. "Wait!"

Rett's powerful legs were crouched, ready to spring, wings poised for flight.

Noah didn't dare look away, pinned to the front seat by the creature's piercing gaze. He exhaled a shaky breath and released the death grip he had on the steering wheel, slowly easing out of the car. He ducked, arms thrown up in reflex, as the creature sprang into the air, wings pitching over him in a huge swath of black.

Gabriel was out of breath when he reached him. "Are you all right? What happened?"

"What the hell was that thing?" Noah rasped, finding his voice. He spun around, a slow 360-degree circle, searching the sky, finding nothing but a charcoal gathering of clouds on the horizon and the muted silver of an overcast sky.

"Noah." Gabriel seemed poised for flight himself and Noah studied him closely, eyes sharp on his pallid face.

"You called it a name. What *was* that thing?"

"Noah," Gabriel said again, placating, and Noah shook off the hand he laid on his forearm.

"No, God damn it, you tell me the truth." He raked fingers through

39

his hair, shaky, anxious, that odd feeling of being watched suddenly back with a vengeance, along with a rush of déjà vu. He whipped his head around to the house and shouted, voice furious and dark. "You get your ass out here, you freakish sonofoabitch! Face me like a man!"

"Rett," Gabriel said softly. "His name is Rett."

Noah's hands tightened into fists as he the weeds again for movement, although he had a sneaking suspicion no more alligators would brave the yard today. "You didn't pull me from the swamp, did you."

Gabriel watched Noah's shoulder's tense in the gloomy light as a fine mist began to fall. He started when Noah spun around.

"Did you?"

Gabriel shook his head. "No."

Noah shoved his index finger in his face. "I'm going to go put my God damn jeans on and then *you*," he jabbed Gabriel in the chest. "Are going to explain a few things." He sidestepped the smaller man's quiet form, whipping around when he reached the corner to yell into sky. "I'm going to put my pants on now, show's over!"

Gabriel sighed and glanced at the second floor window where he suspected Rett was likely hiding, where he had always hidden, ignoring life as it passed them both in a sea of decades and changing history. They had seen the world remake itself time and again in the past two centuries, and yet in some ways, Rett was still the man who had sacrificed it all, down to his very soul, forced to live in guilt and penance for sins no one else remembered.

Gabriel slowly made his way back to his little cabin. Noah deserved an answer.

～

In the cabin, Noah stood at the kitchen counter, fully dressed, shirt buttoned, a fresh mug of coffee in his hand. His handsome jaw was stern, green eyes snapping in the soft light.

Gabriel held up a hand in entreaty. "I promise, I'll explain everything. Just," he pursed his lips. "Just listen before you start yelling again, okay?"

Noah snorted, surprising them both before he relaxed the arm he had crossed in front of his chest and reached for the second cup of coffee he'd poured. "Fine. Go."

"Maybe I should start at the beginning," Gabriel said, taking the mug Noah held out to him, an unfamiliar graciousness permeating the small room for the second time that day.

"That's usually a good place to start," Noah said drily.

Gabriel couldn't detect any malice, nor fear, in Noah's steady gaze, which was really altogether shocking considering the previous twenty minutes.

"It's my story. I should be the one to tell it."

They both jerked at the deep voice from the stoop.

Noah stepped back, in spite of his previous bravado. The figure at the door tentatively opened the screen, and Noah was surprised to see fingers pushing aside the pine frame, long and slender, the bones of his wrists delicate below the corded muscle of a very normal-appearing forearm. When he fully emerged from the shadows and into the kitchen, Noah drew in a quick breath.

Up close, the *'creature'* was not what he expected.

He was tall, at least as tall as Noah, with a shock of thick dark hair, coarsely cut and curling, with intense blue eyes. His features were finely sculpted, hard angles and lines, the barest hint of a cleft in his chin. Noah's stomach clenched when his shapely mouth twisted into an angry line, and a. A snap of electricity filled the air, lifting the hair on his arms and Noah wondered if Gabriel felt it too.

The human details, descriptors that Noah's brain allowed him to catalog, to acknowledge, were easy. Maybe because he couldn't yet drag his eyes from the creature's handsome face to the long span of dark feathers still hanging half outside the door.

"Look at me. All of me," the gravelly voice ground out. "You'd be the first, in a very long time."

"Rett," Gabriel murmured, shifting as though he might move between them.

To protect him, Noah thought, mind spinning fruitlessly, trying to catch up. He cleared his throat, trying to control his natural defense mechanisms telling him to *run.* "Turn around."

Rett's eyebrows shot up and he met the green-eyed stranger's steady gaze. The unfamiliar hum from the previous night returned, hanging heavy between them, and he carefully smoothed his expression lest he reveal the turmoil that was taking place right under his skin. He maneuvered more fully into the kitchen and let the screen door close with a soft *thwump.* Then he slowly turned around.

If Noah didn't know better, he'd swear he was dreaming.

Once, as a teenager, he had gone to a drive-through animal safari and he'd been allowed to hold a rehabilitating bald eagle. It had been injured in a fire and the sanctuary was caring for it until it could be rereleased into the wild. The zookeeper had placed a long, heavy glove over his hand and arm for protection and then gently positioned the eagle in place. Noah would never forget the ripple of bone and ligament when the bird's powerful wings had raised over his head, nor the way its intelligent eyes had looked through him, reading him and taking his measure.

Rett's wings were like that eagle's. The large primary feathers were a deep blue-black, more than a foot in length and at least five inches at their widest point. Noah had inched close enough that he could see the translucent shaft threading through the center of each plume. The next longest layer was edged in a silvery grey and tucked into Rett's sides, creating an oddly striped pattern that Noah imagined was pretty damn striking when the wings were fully spread.

Noah's eyes skated lower. The skin of Rett's hips was smooth and tan, glistening with a fine layer of moisture from the misty rain, and Noah had already noted that his chest was the same. *Normal.* But at mid back there lay a fine, dark trail of soft down in the same iridescent shade as the darkest feathers, a holographic sheen over the musculature between where his scapula should lay, traveling up to his neck and disappearing into his hairline. Noah unconsciously stepped closer and Rett tensed, wings drawing in tight, both men freezing for an interminable breath of uncertainty.

"I," Noah swallowed, flushing. "Sorry. I won't touch." But *damn*, he wanted to. His fingers *itched*.

Rett shifted, feathers fluttering nervously.

Noah glanced down and then quickly away, but not before he had taken in the rest of him. He had on a pair of jeans that looked soft and well-worn, slung low across narrow hips and smoothly fitted to a firm backside. His feet were bare.

Noah became immediately conscious of the fact that he was standing unnaturally close. He could *smell* him.

"Are you quite done?" Rett swung around, narrowly avoiding slamming Noah with a wing joint. From the bright flush in his cheeks, it would appear that it *hadn't* been his imagination that he had felt breath along his neck.

Noah took a giant step back. "Yes, of course. Yeah. I mean—I'm done."

"And?" Those piercing blue eyes that had seemed so hesitantly responsive a few seconds ago now raked over Noah's face in an angry glare, but he didn't wait for a response. "You will leave this property as soon as the crossing is clear. And you will never speak of what you've seen here."

Noah blinked. "Now wait a minute—"

"No!" Rett slammed a fist against the counter and both Noah and Gabriel jumped. "You will leave, or by the grace of God or the devil himself I will *make* you leave."

He shoved through the back door before Noah could come up with a suitably indignant retort.

Noah dragged the back of his hand across his mouth in frustration. He glanced at Gabriel, still cowering by the living room door. "He always that pleasant?"

Gabriel sighed heavily. "Mostly, yes."

Noah laughed, caught off guard by his honesty. He scratched his chin thoughtfully. "I still didn't get his *story*." He air quoted for emphasis.

"Well then you'd better sit down," Gabe smiled. "And I'll fix us a snack. This may take a while."

~

Noah climbed the curved staircase in the waning light, trying to imagine the mansion in her prime. The windows were drapeless, although he supposed there was little need for privacy out here in the swamp; who would dare venture into this old haunt? Resident winged beast notwithstanding.

He stopped at a window on the first landing, imagining the long ago scene Gabriel had described to him. It was surreal; too impossible to be a literal historical retelling and yet...

Somewhere above him wandered a creature that *looked* and *sounded* like a man. With wings.

Noah knew Gabriel was omitting pieces of the story, whether from a sense of loyalty to Rett, or because the knowledge was potentially dangerous in the wrong hands. He bristled at the thought that *he* might be considered a risk. He instinctively knew the truth probably lay hidden somewhere between the words Gabriel had woven in his lyrical tale, and the eyes of the man he called Rett. For now, Noah was content to sleep on it.

He had spent the remainder of the afternoon tinkering with the car and assessing the damage, one eye on the overgrowth separating him from the swamp. He would need either a wrecker or a decently-stocked auto parts store, because his basic emergency kit of tools from the trunk was not going to be enough to get his car running again on his own.

He spent the evening arguing with Gabe about the likelihood of repairing the crossing by mid-week so they could take the old truck into the nearest town. George would be good to assume Noah had holed up somewhere to wait out the storm for a day or two, but longer than that and he would start worrying. Noah needed to get to a phone. And a town, but a phone would solve his most pressing problem.

Well, he mused. His most pressing problem was finding a bed without getting attacked by a giant bird. Man. *Birdman*. He hid his smirk behind his fingers, just in case.

The old house creaked and groaned as he climbed the remaining steps and he wondered belatedly if he believed in ghosts. Old place like this, all those lost souls? The house was permeated with death and after Gabriel's storytime (and a timely whistle of cool air brushing against the back of his neck), he quickly decided he wasn't going to think about *that*.

It hadn't taken much to convince Gabriel that it made no sense for Noah to kick the man out of his own bed two nights in a row just because he happened to be stranded here for another night. Not when there was a conveniently adjacent (veritably empty) mansion.

Rett would never even know he was there.

"He'll know, and he won't like it. Mark my words," Gabe had mumbled, sliding their dinner dishes into the sudsy water with more force than necessary.

"So? What's he going to do? Brood me to death?" Noah smiled his most charming smile when Gabe turned to argue and the priest chuckled.

"You're impossible, Noah Hix. God go with you." And he had waved Noah out the back door with a wet hand.

Noah ran his palm along the smooth wooden banister as he crossed the second floor landing, imagining the hands that had carved it, sanding and polishing the wood until it gleamed; the carpenters who had installed it, painting the spindles a creamy white. The little girl Gabe had said once lived here, who liked to slide down the curve on her backside, into her laughing daddy's arms.

Noah wondered what had happened to that little girl, after her daddy turned into a monster.

That was one part of the story Gabe had definitely skimmed over.

He paused outside of one of the doors in the narrow hallway, listening, still. Dust motes floated in his peripheral vision and a floorboard creaked somewhere to his right; Rett, in his rooms.

Brooding, probably.

He reached for the dark brass knob and eased it over, pushing the door open with a loud groan. He winced as the sound echoed off the tall ceiling. So much for Operation Covert Sleep.

"What do you think you are doing?" Rett's growl was deep and entirely too close, having appeared on Noah's left, rather than from the right like he expected. Hot breath fanned across his cheek.

Noah backed away from the door and held up the flat of his palm in defense, tone soothing. "I'm looking for an empty bed. Care to point me in the right direction?"

"Get out," Rett spat, low and menacing, eyes deepening to indigo in the dim light.

Noah felt a sliver of fear lace up his spine.

For all that he looked like a man, this was no longer a man and hadn't been in two centuries. He should probably remember that.

He took another step backward. "Calm down." He stumbled when Rett advanced on him and he cursed under his breath, face heating in embarrassment. He was a God damn *soldier*. And he sure as hell wasn't about to be bullied by a—

The loud crack of splitting wood was Noah's only warning before there was nothing but a sickening emptiness at his back. His stomach ricocheted into his throat as his body broke through the rotten banister, his breath escaping in a *whoosh* when he was brought up short as Rett caught him by the wrist.

Their eyes held, Noah dangling thirty feet over the marble foyer, Rett crouched on the floor of the landing, one hand vise tight around Noah's arm. Rett grunted and began to pull, his face turning red with the effort, wings spreading wide to assist in leveraging Noah's deadweight. As soon as he was able, Noah hooked a knee over the broken spike of a spindle, and Rett gave one last sharp tug, toppling him to the floor in a heap.

Noah knelt there, on hands and knees, breathing through his nose to calm his racing heart. He peered up at Rett, who was bent at the waist and breathing just as hard.

"You're stronger than you look," he said, not sure whether or not he should be embarrassed when the words ended on a wheeze.

Rett straightened, grimacing as he shook out his hands, fists clenching open and closed. "You're not as smart as you look."

Noah rocked back on his heels, peering over the edge to the floor below, before he stood and moved a safe distance away. He hoped he hid the little shudder that wriggled through his body. He glanced over, licking his lips. "You think I look smart?"

Rett huffed and bit the inside of his cheek. "Not at the moment, no."

Noah swallowed his own grin and stuck out a hand. "Noah Hix. Truce?"

Rett stared at it for a beat before he closed his fingers around Noah's.

Their eyes met and Noah felt his nerves snap to attention, followed by a wash of disappointment when Rett dropped his hand.

"A truce seems fair if you're going to insist on trying to kill yourself while on my land."

Noah blinked, the words taking a moment to register. "Kill my—. I did not," he declared hotly. "How is an alligator my fault? Or uh, uh, a flood!"

"You drove willingly across a clearly dangerous and water-covered passage."

'Because *you* wouldn't let me in the house!"

"That was not me, that was Gabriel."

"Oh, shut up." Noah threw his hands up in disgust. "Gabriel does whatever you tell him to. Don't try to stand there and tell *me* that you didn't tell him to get rid of me."

"That doesn't negate the fact that you attempted to drown."

"Attempted to," Noah sputtered, wondering if he could get a solid punch in before the bastard knocked him to the ground with his giant, creepy wing.

"Rett? Is everything all right?" Gabriel stood at the bottom of the steps. He frowned at the wide section of missing banister, broken pieces littering the foyer floor. "What happened?"

"Noah fell off the landing."

"Noah was practically *pushed* off the landing," Noah grumbled under his breath.

"I told you we should have replaced that banister."

"Ah ha!" Noah crowed, jabbing a finger in Rett's direction.

Rett stared blandly until Noah lowered his arm. He glanced down at Gabriel. "Noah will be staying here tonight. Good night, Gabe."

"All right," Gabriel said hesitantly. He peered up at Noah, eyes narrowing. "You'll call if you need anything."

Noah cocked his head. "And by *call,* you mean literally stick my head out the window and yell, right?"

Gabe chuckled. "Essentially, yes."

"That's what I thought," Noah sighed. "Will do, padre. G'night." He gave a little wave and turned to find Rett had disappeared. "And good night to you too, Mr. Personality," he muttered.

He ignored the first door he had attempted to open (although *that* bared further investigating in the bright light of day), and wandered further into the depths of the house, hopefully far away from his bristly host, and toward a suitable bed.

CHAPTER 5

*N*oah was disoriented when he awoke, a pale, grey light streaming across his face, warming his skin in the already humid room. He blinked rapidly and struggled to sit up, blearily choosing the dusty chest of drawers under the window as a focal point while he shook off the last remnants of sleep.

The previous day flooded back and he sighed, scrubbing his face with his hands. Last night, he had lain looking up at the ornately carved ceiling medallions, wondering if the past twenty-four hours had been a dream. If even now maybe he was tucked away in a hospital ward somewhere, with a massive head injury, his mind having created an elaborate fantasy, influenced by a brutally dark storm and a malevolent mansion on the bayou.

But apparently, judging by a strong caffeine craving and a pretty serious need to pee, he wasn't dreaming. Or if he was, he was damn good at vivid imagery.

He stretched, wincing at the crick in his neck from a strange pillow. He could really use a long hot shower and a pile of pancakes. And coffee. Lots of coffee. Throwing off the blanket, he padded across the room to the window.

At least it wasn't raining. And the water levels looked like they may have receded since the previous day too; maybe Gabriel's truck would be able to clear the crossing by the weekend after all.

The walls and floor seemed to settle around him, unaccustomed to an occupant, creaking and groaning in that way old houses have. Noah grabbed his boots from beside the bed and left the quiet room. The silence was vaguely disconcerting, no electronic hum of appliance or gadgetry or even light bulb. He could use a little human interaction.

Or not so human.

The hallway didn't seem quite so long as it had the night before. He had slept, soundly, in the last bedroom on the floor, in a wide four-poster bed with clean linens that smelled of sunshine and green grass. It had given him pause, the bed so recently made up, as if for a visitor.

At the bottom of the stairs Noah noted that the mess from the previous night had been cleared away, the splintered pieces of wood gone, the floor freshly swept. He wandered through the ground floor, finding the kitchen and pantry easily enough, but a bathroom proving somewhat more difficult.

Surely even winged men needed indoor plumbing, he mused, before giving up in favor of the back yard and a quick wash afterward in the kitchen sink.

RETT SAT UP, awake in an instant, heart pounding.

Something was off.

He jumped out of bed and was across the room and through the door before he registered the faint pulsing of a word in his head. *Noah.* He stood on the landing torn between checking on his charismatic and irritating houseguest and fleeing through the front doors, flying until his head was clear and his blood was calm.

His hand was holding the knob, escape imminent, when he realized what had woken him.

Bacon.

∼

"So you're up." Noah neatly flipped a pancake in a cast iron skillet.

"What are you doing?"

The words were flat, Noah would even dare say menacing, although the delivery was hampered somewhat by the briefest flick of Rett's tongue along his bottom lip. He hid his smile. *Gotcha.*

"I'm making breakfast," he winked, eyes twinkling.

Rett grunted in response, shifting uneasily in the doorway.

"There's a plate for you on the table if you'll stop squirming." Noah walked to said plate and slid the pancake on top of a stack already in place. "You make me nervous," he said bluntly, spatula paused midair.

Rett's mouth fell open, the tips of his ears burning. *Charismatic and irritating.* "I apologize."

Noah had to bite back another grin when the man's feathers literally ruffled. "Apology accepted. Now sit down and dig in." He turned away from the table to finish with the pancake batter. "It's my *thanks for saving my life again* peace offering," he threw over his shoulder. *And for not killing me in my sleep,* he thought wryly, although the more time he spent in Rett's presence, the less threat he could sense. He heard the chair scrape across the floor and settle with Rett's weight.

Noah took a long pull from his mug of coffee and belatedly realized he hadn't offered Rett any.

He snorted softly and poured a second mug, setting the cup in front of the man currently frowning at the plate of food. Rett's dark hair was askew and his cheeks were faintly pink, and damn if Noah didn't find him strangely charming in the morning sun. He picked up the bottle of maple syrup he'd found in the cupboard beside the fridge (a vintage bulbous style that he'd last seen the likes of in Dave's basement), and drizzled it over the pancakes.

"Say when."

Rett's frown deepened. "When what?"

Noah chuckled and twisted his wrist to cut off the flow. "That looks like a good start. Now eat. Your pissy examination of some quality breakfast food is going to hurt the cook's feelings."

"I apologize," Rett repeated stiffly, and picked up a fork.

Noah sat down across from him and tilted his head. "Why are you apologizing?" He chomped off half a piece of bacon in one bite and chewed thoughtfully, studying Rett's hands as the other man primly cut a triangle of pancake, dipping it in the syrup before closing his lips around the fork. His grumpy expression melted instantly into one that came pretty darn close to ecstasy, giving Noah a too quick glimpse of a dimple in his left cheek. Noah realized he was staring and cleared his throat. *Great.* Now *his* cheeks were pink. "Don't you ever wear a shirt?" he muttered irritably.

Rett's wings expanded behind him instantaneously, rattling the silverware on the table.

Noah's eyes widened; the span was at least ten feet.

Rett continued to eat, cutting another triangle of pancake, chewing calmly.

"Fair enough," Noah said under his breath, and popped the rest of the bacon in his mouth.

They ate the remainder of their breakfast in the uneasy silence of the quiet kitchen, the scrape of a fork across a plate or the rustle of a linen napkin the only sounds.

Noah tried not to stare at the elegant fingers handling the fine old silver, both utensils and manners far more refined than what he typically found himself in the company of.

Rett tried to tune out the edgy movements of the man across the table.

Noah finished first and hesitated, wracking his brain for any meager scrap of dining etiquette he might have picked up in his travels. Unfortunately, mess halls and pubs weren't known for their decorum. He settled for watching Rett finish, giving up on the not staring thing because as the sun shifted higher in the sky, a ray of light slanted through the window, dancing along the edges of one of his wings.

The color was incredible, not blue and not black, with an unusual sheen that Noah thought might be green if he would move just a little to the right.

Rett cleared his throat pointedly and Noah started. *Damn.*

"Sorry, man," he smiled ruefully, shrugging in apology. "Wings."

Rett snorted, surprising them both. "Why are you apologizing?" He tossed Noah's earlier question back to him.

"Because you make me nervous," Noah repeated with a grin and the atmosphere in the kitchen immediately warmed.

When they both stood at the same time, they glanced at each other and laughed self-consciously. Rett helped Noah clear the table, and it was an awkward dance of bodies and personal space negotiation, Rett taking up more room than Noah was accustomed to, but also seemingly unaware of Noah's discomfort when he moved too close. Or rather, Noah's *lack* of discomfort with that and an increasing inability to interpret it.

He really wanted to touch those wings.

The sink full, dishes soaking, Rett fidgeted nervously again, poised to flee; Noah was a little surprised he could read him so easily.

"Big plans today?" He asked nonchalantly, selfishly wanting to hold him just a little while longer, see if he could coax that dimple out again.

"What? No. Gardening."

The fact that this was stated so seriously and with such cool composure was the only thing that kept Noah from cracking a joke. Instead, he slid his hands into the soapy water, immediately hissing when the suds hit a cut on the back of his wrist.

"What's wrong?" Rett tensed, alert, unconsciously stepping forward.

Noah shook his hand free of the soap and grimaced. "One of those damn chickens pecked me when I was trying to get an egg." He held up his wrist for inspection, the small slash visibly reddened. "It's nothing. I just forgot."

When Rett didn't respond, he looked over to find the other man fighting what Noah suspected might be a legitimate, fully-fledged smile. "What?"

"A chicken." Rett lost the battle and laughed softly, but he at least had the grace to partially hide his amusement behind a palm.

"A broody hen," Noah corrected, wishing he would move his

fingers and let him see that smile. He pointed a sudsy finger at Rett. "Which, *you* would know a thing or two about."

Rett straightened with a frown. "Beg pardon?"

Noah huffed, shaking his head. So much for his long-withstanding ability to quip his way out of uncomfortable situations. "Nevermind."

"You may," Rett hesitated, head canting to the right, eyes shifting away from Noah's when he glanced over. "You could help? In the garden?"

It was a question, but also an olive branch, and Noah recognized it as such. "I'm not really much in the way of green thumbs, Rett. But maybe. I'm going to gauge the depth of the water first, see how close she is to crossing."

"Do not go into the bayou," Rett was instantly tense again, his already perfect posture rigid, jaw set.

"Relax," Noah chuckled. "No suicide attempts today." He winked when Rett remained hovering in the doorway. "Promise."

"I will leave you, then," Rett said stiffly, formal again. "Thank you for breakfast."

"You're welcome," Noah said, but he knew by the rustle of feathers the words fell on an empty room. He sighed and reached for a towel to dry his hands. One of these days he was going to be the one to have the last word.

GABE PEERED INTO THE KITCHEN, sighing in relief when he spotted Noah at the refrigerator. "Good morning," he offered, gently closing the door behind him. He sniffed in surprise. "You cooked."

Noah grinned. "I did. I'd offer you some but we ate it all." He scratched the back of his neck thoughtfully. "And that was pretty rude. Sorry."

"You ate. You and Rett."

Gabe's blank look tickled Noah in ways he couldn't quite comprehend. "Me and Rett," he confirmed.

Gabe's mouth worked open and closed before he gave up and expelled a long rush of air. "I don't know what to say."

Noah's eyes narrowed on his shocked face. "Apparently you're trying to say one of us," he jabbed his finger toward the empty house to indicate its primary occupant, "was in danger of not making it down for breakfast." He shut the refrigerator door. "I'm assuming you weren't worried about the fella with the feathers."

"I wasn't worried," Gabe rushed to assure Noah, although his twitchy mannerisms were wholly unconvincing. "Not about your safety."

"You're a terrible liar," Noah laughed. "But I'll forgive you if you let me use your bathroom. I would love a shower."

"There's no shower." Gabe sighed in relief. Noah and Rett had apparently both weathered the night well. And the morning. "But you are welcome to the bathtub." He hesitated before offering a second choice. "You could use Rett's shower. It's quite large."

"Rett has a shower." Now it was Noah's turn to wear a vacant expression.

Gabe laughed. "Yes. And it's *very* impressive. His size requirements compelled an unusual design."

Noah blinked twice. And then twice more. He knew the former priest wasn't trying to torture him with visions of a very naked, very winged Rett, *wet*, but once that image was lodged in his head he had a feeling it would be a long time before he expelled it. "Ahh, maybe just the tub today," he said gruffly.

"Of course," Gabe said, oblivious to Noah's discomfort. "Do you have clothing in your car? I'd be happy to add your laundry to my own."

Noah followed him out the back door and down the steps. "Yeah, about that. Where do you get your clothes, anyway? Those are definitely not vintage."

"Television," Gabe murmured.

"You like TV, padre?" Noah asked, grinning.

"No," Gabe shook his head quickly. "I," he swallowed. "I have a small set. I watch the news."

"Liar," Noah grinned. He bumped their shoulders together. "So what's your poison? Daytime talk shows?" He wiggled his eyebrows. "Dancing with the Stars?" Gabe flushed, waving him off, and Noah laughed, spinning around and heading in the opposite direction. "Clothes," he said. "Be right back."

He retrieved his duffle from the trunk, shading his eyes and peering into the sky. He wondered how often and how far Rett flew. This was an isolated area of the country, to be sure, but he imagined it still held a danger for a creature trying to remain hidden and undiscovered. He glanced at the second floor windows of the mansion, wondering if maybe Rett was showering.

Nope. Nopenopenope, he thought, frantically humming the opening lines of John Denver's *Thank God I'm a Country Boy* to deflect that image-laden mine field.

He was still chuckling at his brain's perplexing choice of song a few minutes later when he ducked into Gabe's little house.

IN FULL SUN, the feathers had a definite green sheen.

Noah only knew this because he had stumbled upon one as he walked across the yard, angling toward the far northern corner where he could see Rett kneeling in the dirt. He turned the feather over in his hand, holding it to the light and studying the shifting hues. He held it suspended over the thick overgrowth, meaning to drop it into the grass, but changed his mind at the last minute and tucked it into his hip pocket instead.

He could see the instant Rett knew he was approaching because his wings raised, on guard, waiting. Deciding he had been getting the most honest reactions by forcing an element of surprise, Noah squatted in the dirt beside him.

"Noah Hix, reporting for duty." He was rewarded by the unguarded look of surprise Rett shot him.

Rett recovered quickly. "I am unsure I should accept your assistance. I would like to eat this winter."

Noah laughed. "Ouch. I said I didn't have a green thumb, not that I was completely inept. I have skills."

"I am sure that you do," Rett murmured.

Noah glanced sharply at the handsome face, something fluttering to life in his midsection at the husky tone, but Rett busied himself snipping off a low-lying branch on the rose bush he tended. "So you eat roses? Is that a delicacy for your kind or a personal dietary quirk?"

"You would amuse me more if you would take up that pair of shears and help," Rett replied calmly. *Snip.*

Noah snorted. "Stop with the nosy ass questions, Noah. Got it."

Snip.

"You weren't being nosy," Rett said carefully after a moment. "I eat food."

Noah chuckled and sat back on his butt in the dirt, deciding he'd rather watch than participate. "I know that, Rett. I fed you, remember?" He rested his forearms on his knees.

Rett picked up the second pair of shears and held them out, meeting Noah's gaze. "I remember."

Noah fought the urge to shiver. *Damn.* Rett's deep rumble, the blue of his eyes, the sun on their backs, and the casual intimacy with which they sat together on the ground combined at once to give Noah a jolt of nerves.

He thought, inexplicably, of the feather in his pocket. He wondered if it carried the same warm, mellow scent that listed over him as a breeze fluttered by.

"My daughter's," Rett said, interrupting Noah's crazy train of thought.

"Huh?" Noah resisted the urge to scoot closer. Or maybe farther away. He wasn't entirely sure which would slake the puzzling spike of *want* now simmering in his gut. He accepted the shears, but their fingers very carefully did not graze.

"The roses. I planted them on the day she was born."

Noah tore his eyes from the messy spikes of dark hair and looked at the thorny bushes in front of him. The last blooms of the season were full and lush, a deep, dark pink. It took him a moment before the math hit him.

"Wait a minute, these are two hundred years old?" He sat up straight. *No way.*

Rett laughed softly and trimmed away another errant branch. "Thereabouts." He sighed and the sound was wistful. "I fear they aren't for this world much longer, however. They no longer respond to careful monitoring. Perhaps their time here is done."

It was the longest string of words Rett had spoken to him and it took Noah a moment to parse through their melodic tones to comprehend his meaning. "They're dying."

"Yes," Rett said. He laid the shears on the ground. "So you can see why I would prefer you not hasten their demise," he deadpanned.

It took Noah four seconds to register the twinkle in his eyes.

"Funny," he said dryly. "Where are you going?" he asked when Rett rolled deftly to his feet.

"To check the squash."

"Squash?" Noah grimaced. *No thank you.* "Hey, Rett?" he asked after a few more moments lazily soaking up the sun.

"Hmm?"

Noah studied the man bent over the green vines, wondering vaguely if he was about to destroy whatever truce they seemed to have forged. But he had had an idea while he bathed in Gabe's tiny bathroom and, well, the day was not getting any younger. "Do you think you could fly me over the bayou? Drop me on the other side?"

Rett straightened, and from his rod-stiff bearing, Noah knew he was correct in assuming it would be a sensitive request. He had a feeling Rett didn't venture over the bayou often.

"You would like to leave." Rett moved to a new plant and picked a fat, yellow squash, dropping it to the grass beside the other vegetables.

"Well, yeah. I'd like to go home," Noah offered, using his knee as leverage to assist himself off the ground. "But I need to fix my car first. At least find a phone. Let my brother know I'm alive." He tried not to feel slighted when Rett moved away from him as he approached. "Gabe said it wasn't more than five or six miles."

"Seven," Rett said, quietly dropping another squash to the ground.

"Seven," Noah huffed. "Do you think you could do that for me?" He jumped when Rett straightened, his wings expanding and fluttering abruptly, preparing, Noah realized, for flight. "Wait a minute," he laughed, holding out a hand. "I need to go grab my wallet."

When he emerged from under the shade of Gabe's porch a few minutes later, he could see Rett waiting by the crossing.

"Noah," Gabe stopped him with a hand on his arm. "I don't have to tell you, ask you—"

"I won't say anything," Noah broke in, his eyes on the far away figure by the water. "I'll be back by dark." He left before Gabe could respond.

When he reached the edge of the crossing, murky water rushing by, high and fast and frustratingly deep, he grinned sheepishly at the man standing in the shadow of a cypress, looking for all the world like a fantasy novel come to life. "I'm afraid of heights. And I never fly."

Rett pushed off of the tree trunk and approached him slowly. If Noah didn't know better, he might even say *stealthily.*

"Close your eyes."

Noah did, and didn't scrutinize his hasty compliance too closely.

He was weightless and then he was not, and when he was *not,* he was flat on his back, skidding across the gravel and dirt. He coughed, groaning as he rolled to prop himself on an elbow. He glared across the bayou where his *flight aid* had already returned, his retreating outline framed by the decaying mansion in the background.

"Don't wait up!" he called sarcastically, wincing at the raw soreness of his backside as he climbed to his feet. He brushed off his jeans and grimaced at the long, empty road in front of him. "Seven miles," he muttered and began to walk.

Gabriel found Rett standing by the Road Runner, studying the car's dark hood as if he stared hard enough, long enough, he might decipher the enigma of the man it belonged to.

"Well that," Rett said softly, "is that."

Gabe looked up at him in surprise. "You don't think he'll be back? He seemed awfully attached to this car."

"Would you come back, if you could escape?"

Rett's bleak look held more emotion than Gabe had seen from him in a very long time.

"Rett," he murmured.

"I'm going to tend the roses."

"Rett," Gabriel tried again, reaching for his friend and missing, Rett's movements too fluid, too graceful, a weightless dance across the overgrown grasses until he was a distant figure backlit by the sun.

CHAPTER 6

The town of Revelation appeared out of the deep green landscape gradually; a house here, a farm there, a gas station, a quiet park, until Main Street loomed ahead. Downtown was a throwback to mid-century America, behind each tall building facade a classic rectangular shape of brick and mortar.

He passed a red and white barbershop pole, smiled at a girl sitting at a café table outside of a coffee shop, and spotted Bloom's Hardware a few doors down. There was a spiffy green lawn mower parked out front, a lively *Sale!* sign on the seat, and flats of perennials on a tall wire shelf flanking the windows. The overhead bell pealed when he pushed open the door and stepped into the cool, dim interior.

"Be right with you," a voice called from the back of the store.

"No hurry," Noah tossed in the direction of the voice. The aisles at the front of the store were full of paint cans and painting supplies, a knee-to-ceiling display of colorful swatches taking up the majority of one wall. He spotted the automotive section near the back of the store and picked his way around the crowded displays surrounding a glass case holding the cash register.

An aproned man, rotund and jovial with a shiny bald head and silvery side burns greeted him just as he rounded the corner to look at spark plugs.

"Can I help you find anything?" He held out his hand expectantly and Noah shook it, smiling at the small town charm.

"Thanks. Just picking up a few things to do some repairs." He grinned ruefully and scratched his chin. "I got caught in the storm a couple nights ago and flooded my engine."

The man tsked, shaking his head in sympathy. "Happens often in these parts, unfortunately. Where are you from, son?"

"Kansas City," Noah replied. "Was just passing through when she hit."

"You're lucky," the man said somberly. "We lost a couple of good people that night in the flood." He held out his hand again. "Fred Bloom."

"Noah Hix."

"Did you try and turn over the engine?"

"Yeah," Noah said, head cocked when Fred frowned. "Why?"

Fred shook his head. "Might have blown your engine then, depending on how deep the water was. You'll need to pull all the spark plugs, replace all the fluids and filters." He started perusing the aisle, mumbling to himself as he rifled through drawer of well-worn repair books. "Probably drain the gas and flush the lines too. What kind of car did you say it was?"

"Sixty-nine Plymouth Road Runner." Noah bit his lip, pounding a fist silently against his thigh. *Of course.* He should have known better than to try and start her after she'd been submerged. Assuming she *had* been submerged. He still hadn't gotten the full story out of Gabriel about that.

Fred whistled, a gleam in his eye when he glanced over with a grin. "Now that's a car. And bless her, too. Those newfangled pieces of horse shit don't tolerate the barest hint of dampness."

Noah snorted and relaxed his fist. Maybe he hadn't completely fucked his baby up.

Fred dug a little deeper and pulled a manual free in triumph. "Here we go." He passed the booklet to Noah. "That should get you started. Now. Let's fix you up with some supplies."

Noah was ushered through the small but well-stocked automotive section and ended up with two large bags of goods and directions to the nearest diner when his stomach rumbled heartily.

"Benny's is what you're cravin'. He cooks a chicken fried steak that'll make you cry," Fred said in reverence. "And his jambalaya, ooh-eee." He smacked his lips. "My mouth waters just thinkin' about it."

Noah laughed. "I'm not so much a rice man, but I could dig into a chicken fried steak and mashed potatoes."

"Well, Benny's it is, then. You come back and let me see that car when you've got'er running, you hear?"

"Will do." Noah gave a little wave and negotiated the crowded paint aisle to the front of the store. He paused when his eyes fell on the cheery colors of the flowers visible through the window. "Hey, Fred?"

"Yeah?" Fred poked his head around the aisle, peering at Noah with the same friendly smile.

"Do you have any suggestions for a rose bush that's, uh," Noah hesitated, flustered and unsure. He had no idea what symptom's Rett's rose bush was displaying. "Not doing so hot?" he finished lamely.

"Hmm. Not blooming?"

"No, there are blooms." Noah shifted his bags and they bumped against his legs. "It's an old bush," he offered tentatively, hoping like hell Fred didn't ask too many questions.

"Heirloom?" Fred asked, already turning down an aisle with a vibrantly painted *Garden* sign hanging above it. He popped back around the corner when Noah didn't immediately follow. "They smell real good? Like grandma's roses?" He winked and Noah chuckled.

"Yeah. They smell nice." Noah felt his cheeks warm and glanced at the door.

"Try this," Fred said, startling Noah when he appeared at his side. He held out a green and yellow box. "Mix two scoops with a gallon of water and feed your bush once a week. Should perk up in no time. But if not," he wagged a finger at Noah. "You come back and I'll get out the big guns."

Noah laughed again and accepted the box. "How much?"

"On the house. You just bring that handsome car of yours round so I can take her for a spin around the block, capisce?"

"You got it," Noah said, backing out of the door, bell ringing merrily as he stepped into the bright afternoon sun. "Thanks, Fred." The man was already hustling to the back of the store, his hand thrown up in a jaunty, backwards wave.

Noah started down the sidewalk and stopped in awe a half a block later when he spotted a payphone mounted against a brick wall. He hadn't seen a model like this since he was a kid. He carefully set the bags at his feet and dug through his pockets for all his change. "Here goes nothin'," he muttered, dialing George's number.

The recording instructed him to insert an insane amount to complete the call and he cursed under his breath before he hung up. He wondered if collect calls were still a thing, and picked up the handset, ready to try again. After negotiating with a bored operator, George's voice came on the line a few moments later.

"Noah!"

"Georgie," Noah sighed. "Thank God."

"Where the hell are you? I've been worried sick. Why haven't you been answering your phone?" George's voice fluctuated between anger and fear and Noah grinned.

"Vacationing in the most ridiculous mansion you've ever seen."

"I'm not kidding, Noah. Where are you?"

"Okay, okay, hold onto your panties." Noah pursed his lips. The trick with keeping things from George was to tell a carefully edited version of the truth, because he could notoriously smell a lie, especially if Noah was telling it. "I'm still in Louisiana. Got caught in the storm. My phone's a lost cause." That was accurate enough.

"So are you on your way home? What part of Louisiana? How far did you get?"

"How's Max?" Noah asked, deflecting. "She still puking?"

"Don't change the subject. And she's fine. Food poisoning."

"We all ate the same things," Noah said incredulously.

"Yeah, well, apparently you and I have iron stomachs. She's on the mend now. Feeling guilty because we thought you were lying in a ditch somewhere."

Not too far from the truth, Noah thought. "Nah, I'm okay. But the car's in rough shape. She flooded a little. It'll be a few days til I have her dried out and running."

George was silent and Noah fidgeted. "You still there? This call ain't cheap."

"You called me collect, Noah. That means I'm paying." George's voice was amused and Noah relaxed.

"Just looking out for your budget-conscious ass. Can you let Dave know I'll be a few days later than planned?"

"Sure," George said, and Noah could hear the hesitancy in his voice. "You sure you're okay? You don't need me to fly down? Or bring the wrecker? We could tow the car back."

"No," Noah said and if the protest was too quick, or held too much intensity, he ignored it and prayed George would do the same. "I can handle it. She'll be good to go in a few days."

"And your phone? Do you have a number where I can reach you?"

Noah bit his lip. "Ah, I'll have to stop by the store and grab a throwaway I guess. I'll call you as soon as I have a number."

"Okay, but—"

"Oh would you look at the time," Noah interrupted. "Time is money, Georgie. I'll call you later."

"Noah!"

Noah hung up the phone with a smile. George would be cursing him the rest of the night. His stomach growled again and he retrieved his sacks from the sidewalk. Time to eat.

BENNY'S WAS one of those deep-fried, homecooked oases Noah loved to sniff out on old two-lane highways and in backwater towns. The waitresses wore pastel uniforms with dainty white pocket squares, and the cook leaned over the window separating the kitchen and the counter with a lazy smile and a deep Southern twang.

"Paula, you gonna get this meatloaf special out to those fine folks in that booth over there or am I gonna have to fire your pert butt?"

"Benny, the day you fire someone is the day pigs fly," a brassy blonde retorted, taking the plates from his hands and sashaying her way across the polished checkered floor.

Noah surveyed the scene with a quick glance and decided to take a seat at the counter. He slid onto a red pleather stool and tucked his packages under his feet.

"Well, hello stranger. What can I do you for?" This waitress was a redhead, her heart-shaped face nearly overwhelmed by big green eyes. She tapped a pencil against the side of her glossy mouth as she gave Noah the onceover.

"We feed the customers, Maisy, we don't eat them," Benny drawled from his perch in the window. "You don't have to take any sass from her, mind you," he said to Noah with a wink. "Just shoo her off if she gets too fresh."

"Benny, shut up," Maisy protested, but her eyes never left Noah's face, and the words were delivered with an inviting grin.

Noah answered it with one of his own. "I'm just here for the chicken fried steak. And," he nodded toward the glass-covered cake stands on the counter. "Maybe some of that pie?"

"Mashed potatoes or fries?" Maisy asked efficiently.

"Mashed."

"Pecan or apple?" Maisy scribbled across her pad.

"Two of each."

Maisy's eyebrows shot up to her hairline.

"To go," Noah amended. "And you'd better double the chicken fried steak too."

"That's quite an appetite you got there, stranger," Benny noted, taking the slip of paper from Maisy's fuchsia-tipped fingers.

Noah shrugged. "I heard it was the best I'll ever taste."

"Damn straight," the cook grinned, tipping his hat and shoving off the window. He disappeared into the kitchen.

Noah relaxed on the bar stool, gratefully accepting a cup of coffee from the redhead even though he hadn't asked for it, content to people watch while he waited.

~

THE WALK back to seemed twice as long and Noah cursed the humid heat that settled over him, thick and wet, his t-shirt sticking in patches of dampness, rivulets of sweat running into his eyes. He wished he had accepted a ride from the truck that had stopped about three miles back, but he would have felt funny asking them to drop him off anywhere close to the mansion. He sighed in relief when he spotted the big old house through the tree line and shifted the cardboard box that contained all of his purchases. Benny the cook had insisted he transfer his bags to the box when he found out Noah was on foot, swearing *those flimsy ass plastic sacks will never hold up.*

Now he just had to figure out how to get Rett or Gabe's attention from this side of the bayou.

~

RETT STUDIED A THORNY LEAF CAREFULLY, inspecting a brownish spot near the edge, wondering if it was a fungus or perhaps the result of an insect. The roses had not bloomed as significantly this season, decreasing incrementally each year, although the fragrant pink blossoms were still heavy and sweet on the branches. He touched the rippling edge of a petal with a fingertip.

He looked up sharply when a faint whistle carried over the rustle of the trees. His eyes widened when he spotted Noah on the other side of the waterway, arms full and a wide grin on his handsome face.

He brushed the dirt from his hands and stood, spine straight and stiff.

He swallowed the strange flutter in his throat.

"You mind if I hitch a ride?" Noah called as Rett approached.

Rett studied him through the trees, noting the pink of his cheeks and nose, and the dampness of his forehead, slick with sweat.

"You were gone a long while."

"Seven miles, Rett," Noah said exasperatedly. He moved the box to his hip and frowned. "You gonna wing over here or not?"

"Close your eyes."

"Rett." Noah huffed in frustration. "I can handle it okay? Just get your feathery ass over here. It's hotter'n hell and I'd really like to jump in a cold—" His eyes widened when Rett's wings expanded and he was across the bayou in seconds, dropping mere inches from where Noah stood, moving the thickened air in a quick, heavy draft. He expelled the breath he'd inhaled. "Bath," he finished weakly.

"I prefer to shower. You would enjoy my bathing room, I suspect." Rett's eyes roved over Noah's face, frowning at his sunburned cheeks, holding a lengthy pause on his mouth, before darting away.

In spite of the heat, Noah suppressed a shiver. He started when Rett moved.

"Are you all right?" Rett asked, quirking an eyebrow, hands hovering at Noah's waist.

Noah frowned. For a second there, Rett had looked at his mouth like… He tamped down the strange tickling response his skin to the other man's proximity. "I'm fine. Want to get this show on the road?"

"I," Rett hesitated, studying the box. "I think it would be best if I held you from behind this time."

Noah's stomach dipped at the words, or maybe the hushed tone, too intimate for their open surroundings, and he felt his face flush. He was suddenly thankful for the sun that had surely bloomed a disguising burn over his cheeks. "Sure, whatever," he replied gruffly, shifting slightly on his heel.

Rett carefully finished the rearrangement of their bodies, hands falling lightly above his hips. Noah could feel each slim finger through the thin fabric of his t-shirt and the muscles of his abdomen clenched in a sluggish drag, every cell, every hair, surging to life, poised. Rett's breath fell against the back of his head, each puff blowing coolly through the sweaty hair at his nape. Strong hands tightened, grip firm, before relaxing, fingers spreading wide as they slid achingly slow across Noah's stomach, until two forearms overlapped around his ribcage.

Noah's lungs burned and he realized he was holding his breath.

He blinked, heart tripping when he felt the cool nudge of a nose behind his ear, and then he was weightless, and he slammed his eyes shut as the ground fell away.

"Thanks," he said when he felt solid earth beneath his feet again, hating that his voice was breathless.

"You're welcome." Rett released him and stepped back. Then back again.

Noah pointedly ignored the lingering *itch* along the path where Rett's arms had rested. *Fuck.* "Ahh," he reached into the box and retrieved a white paper sack, anxious to dispel the strange tension. "I brought dinner?"

Rett frowned. "I don't understand."

"Take out? Diner food? Rett, come on. I brought *dinner*. For us."

At Rett's blank look, Noah rolled his eyes and started across the lawn. "Fine. Stay out here and play in the dirt. I'm gonna eat pie."

He peeked behind him to find Rett still standing at the edge of the bayou, but he thought he detected a note of conflict in his somber face. "It's apple," he added nonchalantly, shaking the bag for good measure.

A rush of wind ruffled his hair and when he looked up, Rett was waiting on the porch.

"Show off," he muttered.

CHAPTER 7

The soft light from the oil lamps danced across the blue-black sheen of feathers, drawing Noah's gaze repeatedly, despite how he instinctively understood Rett hated to be exposed. Noah couldn't help it, though. The night was dark and the house was still, except for a soft pattering of rain at the windows; it insulated the two men in the parlor from the rest of the world.

"Stop staring," Rett growled, but the words were less fractious than Noah had come to expect. Or maybe he was getting better at reading between the gruff exterior lines of his prickly host.

The pie had been a revelation, and, regrettably for Noah's libido, a source of new and unexpected frustration.

Rett's blissed out expression at the first taste of fruit and cinnamon on his tongue had rendered Noah speechless. He couldn't even finish his own pie after that, mouth gone dry with illicit consideration, and he was extremely grateful for the table that hid his body's instantaneous response. Every last pinprick of awareness and heat he had endured while standing on that dusty roadside returned with a vengeance, before taking a sharp nosedive into his pants. He discreetly pressed the flat of his palm against his lap as he watched Rett devour first his own slice, and then the rest of Noah's, those deep blue eyes heavy lidded and mouthwateringly sultry in the fading light of the kitchen lamp. Noah had to swallow back a groan when the soft sweet pinkness of Rett's tongue darted out to snatch up the last bits of sugar that clung to the bottom of his lower lip.

It was porn. Pure and simple.

Noah wondered absently if he was suffering from sunstroke, as he moved the book he was unequivocally *not reading* into a position that allowed him to continue staring undetected.

Glossy dark wings were draped over the deep-hued velvet of the wingchair opposite him in the parlor, falling to the floor in a shimmering carpet of feathers. He shifted on the settee self-consciously, his breathing altered ever so slightly by an oddly persistent anxiety.

Suddenly, Rett sucked in a breath and one wing twitched hard, forced out at an awkward angle, rigid.

Noah sat up. "What's the matter? Are you hurt?"

"No," Rett ground out between his teeth. "Cramp." His shoulders were slumped forward, dark head bowed, and the offending wing trembled. "It happens occasionally."

"C'mere." The words were out of his mouth before he knew he was going to say them, but Noah couldn't drag them back.

"What?" Rett's head jerked up, his eyes wide.

"Come here," Noah enunciated carefully, throwing all caution and a healthy dose of common sense by the wayside, scooting back on the settee until there was plenty of room, even on the stupidly tiny sofa. *Where was a giant wraparound sectional when you needed one?* His tossed his unread book to the floor.

Rett studied him in the flickering light until Noah squirmed.

"Fine, stay over there all bitchy and cramped up, it's no skin off my —" Noah's mouth slammed shut when Rett stood and dropped unceremoniously onto the settee in front of him. His lithe hip bumped against Noah's bent knee, and Noah closed his eyes for the space of two heartbeats. When he opened them, Rett had dropped his head on the back of the little couch, the cramped wing pushed close to Noah's hands.

"Please," Rett muttered into the skin of his forearm.

Noah exhaled, awash in the warm scent that was uniquely *Rett*, quite literally surrounded by the very thing he had been dying to get his hands on since the first moment he had laid eyes on Rett Blackburn. His fingers held the faintest tremble as he ran them lightly over the feathers.

They were smooth, sleek. Like silk, but different, because they were alive, moving under his fingertips, clearly stretching, turning in the direction of his touch.

Noah shook his head to clear it. Rett was in pain and Noah was selfishly indulging in a dark little fantasy of feathers and foreplay. He narrowed his gaze on Rett's strong back and the offending wing, finding what appeared to be a hard knot of muscle under the joint where his scapula should be. He pressed into it with two fingers and Rett hissed.

Noah jerked his hand back. "Sorry," he said swiftly, voice husky.

"No," Rett grunted. "Don't stop."

Noah ignored his body's swift reaction to the gravelly command and pressed the heel of his hand against the knot, rotating it in deep circles, urging the mangled muscles to release. Rett moaned, softly, and Noah steeled himself against the sound, silently sending a plea for common sense to his excitable dick. Sweat beaded on his forehead and he swiped at it with the back of his free hand. The muscle was stubborn, intractable like its owner, so Noah came at it from different angles, both hands, the fingers of one massaging the hardness while the other slid around to the front of the wing to rub against the opposing joint.

It was if an electric current jolted through both of them when Noah burrowed his hand into the feathers and Rett's head jerked up with a gasp. Noah tried to withdraw and Rett caught his hand, forcing it back into place, panting. "That's, I've," he was biting his lip and Noah unconsciously shifted closer, Rett's hips now achingly close to his lap. *Dick be damned.*

"Shh, relax," he murmured.

Rett's head tipped forward with a sigh of relief when the knot eased under Noah's ministrations and the wing finally fell, relaxed.

Noah continued to massage the surrounding muscles and cartilage, quelling an absurd urge to place his lips there, wondering how the fine, soft feathers would feel against the skin of his mouth. Then he raced to douse the fire that spurred to life deep within his belly, fought to maintain some semblance of control, praying Rett wouldn't sense his turmoil or his crazy turns of thought. He began to comb through the feathers lightly, paying close attention to any joints, the strange array of muscle that attached the appendages to Rett's back, smiling when a particular swipe of thumb or press of knuckle elicited a breathy moan.

He could touch Rett all night if he would keep making those sounds.

He moved to the opposite side long after the cramp was gone, one wing draped lazily over his leg and down across the floor. His mind wandered as he stroked and petted and he was surprised to realize that in all likelihood no one had touched Rett in approximately two hundred years, which might explain his (very intoxicating) responsiveness.

It likely had nothing to do with Noah, himself.

Rett tensed when Noah absently scratched his fingers down the center of his back, then groaned loud and long.

"You should probably tone it down or the padre is going to get the wrong idea," Noah teased softly, scratching the same long line again, chuckling when Rett shuddered, unconsciously following Noah's hand when it moved away.

"I've had that itch for two hundred years."

Noah froze. "Did you just crack a joke?" He peered over Rett's shoulder with a grin.

"Maybe." Rett's jaw remained stoically firm and Noah fought a sudden desire to run his teeth along it, taste the dark stubble on his tongue. The *want* was so strong, so palpable, he tensed, waiting for Rett to sense the direction of his thoughts and fling Noah aside in disgust.

When Rett remained slumped across the back of the settee, half splayed across Noah's thighs, blissful and unaware, Noah breathed easy again and allowed his fingers more freedom in their exploration, digging deep under the silky firm top feathers and combing into the soft, dark down beneath. When a single feather fell into his lap he sucked in a breath.

"Sorry," he said quickly.

Rett snorted, the sound muffled through the pillow of his arm. "That happens frequently. Keep it."

Noah felt the tips of his ears redden as a blush raced up his neck. So his fascination hadn't gone unnoticed. He carefully laid the feather on the floor beside the settee and returned his hands into the depths of the wings again. Rett sighed contentedly, body visibly pliant. His hip was wedged firmly against Noah's knee, and Noah mused how easy it would be to slide him into the cradle of his legs, pull him tight against his chest, explore other parts of the mysterious creature that was half man, half—

Noah mentally regrouped. *Fuckfuckfuck.*

He gently extracted his hands, ensuring the smooth directional flow of the feathers as he went. "They're very soft, and," he searched in vain for the right word, one that wouldn't sound too infatuated. "Shiny," he finished lamely.

Rett glanced over his shoulder with a sleepy, even look. "You're quite attractive as well."

Noah flushed. "I. I wasn't trying to—" His mouth snapped shut and he tried again. "I wasn't coming on to you, Rett. I was saying I like your wings."

Rett's mouth twitched in amusement and Noah huffed, sliding out from behind him on the sofa, suddenly needing to be far, far removed from spicy scents and warm, smooth skin and silky feathers.

"Noah."

Noah was already half way to the door, embarrassed and hot and achingly hard. But he stopped. Because Rett almost never used his name. "Yeah."

He willed his heart to stop pounding, wondered if Rett could hear it.

"Thank you."

Noah blew out a long, unsteady breath. "You're welcome. Good night."

He didn't wait for Rett to respond and took the stairs two at a time.

CHAPTER 8

Gabriel stood in the doorway of the parlor, the night and storm muting the usual colors and sounds, buffering the old house in the damp smells of the waterway that lingered outside her doors. He watched Rett stare out at the rain, a lamp still burning on the end table, though he knew Rett had no need of it. The flickering flame threw uneven shadows along the faded damask wallpaper behind the settee.

"He's gone up to bed."

Gabe wrinkled his nose at being caught lurking in the shadows again. "I wondered, when you did not show up to dine with me."

Rett turned slightly, his profile strong in the pale gold light of the lamp. "He brought food back with him. I apologize. We should have come for you."

Gabe's eyes narrowed. Was that a smile gracing his stern friend's mouth? "What are you smiling about?"

Rett huffed and waved his hand in dismissal. "There's pie in the refrigerator. Though I fear if you eat all of it, Noah will have terse words for you in the morning."

"Pie?" Gabe leaned against the doorframe, relieved. He had

avoided the house on purpose, hoping that given enough time alone, Noah and Rett might forge a willing and amicable truce.

The intensity of Rett's gaze as it had followed their handsome guest around the grounds had not escaped his notice.

"Apple," Rett said with a wide grin, turning fully into the room.

Gabe blinked at the transformation in Rett's face. He was suddenly, heartbreakingly, youthful. He schooled his own expression carefully, into one of teasing joviality. "I confess I'm quite jealous. Apple pie is my weakness."

"I remember," Rett chuckled softly, staring down at the settee, seemingly lost in thought.

Gabe opened his mouth to retort when a crash from overhead shook the quiet darkness, followed immediately by a gut-wrenching wail.

Rett shoved him aside and was at the top of the dark landing before Gabe reached the foyer.

"Stay there," he ordered, disappearing in the direction of Noah's room.

Noah thrashed on the bed, legs tangled in his sheets, as he fought an invisible enemy, his throat emitting guttural moans. Rett leaned over him with one knee on the bed, a gentle hand on his shoulder, intent on waking him.

Noah's left hook landed squarely on his jaw, knocking Rett's head back with the force of the impact. Rett grunted and tightened his grip on Noah's arm, dodging the next swing efficiently and throwing his body weight over the struggling man, pinning his wayward fists between their chests.

"Noah."

Noah blinked rapidly in the dark, jaw clenched tight, teeth grinding audibly in the sudden stillness. "Rett," he finally breathed. His eyes fluttered closed and he tilted his head back on the pillow, shuddering as he released the tight tension in his body.

Rett swallowed. He was suddenly hyperaware of the proximity of his mouth to Noah's throat, and the lingering tremors of the body under his hands; they felt intimate, the ghost of a long-ago lover at the cusp of climax. He licked his lips nervously, torn between fleeing and staying to ensure the danger was over. "Noah," he repeated his name, softer. "Are you all right?"

He moved to retreat after a lengthy moment of silence in which Noah didn't meet his gaze, but one of Noah's hands slid free to grasp at his waist.

"Wait."

Rett froze, the warm fingertips pressed into his side the center of his consciousness, the clean, distinct smell of *Noah* filling his nostrils. He felt a swift and insistent need to *move*.

He slid out of Noah's grasp, putting crucial inches between them, poised on the edge of the mattress. He fought against an instinctual necessity for escape, stilling as Noah watched him from under heavy lids.

"Did I wake you?" Noah asked, voice smoky and deep. He rubbed his eyes. "Sorry."

Rett shook his head once. "I was awake."

Noah watched him in the dark, blinking slowly, the dream fading. It was an old one; fire and smoke, the ground rushing toward him, a sudden blackness buffering the screams of his friends as they burned. He ran an unsteady hand over the feathers draped across his lap, the textures soothing. Rett conspicuously leaned into the touch and he swallowed a smile. Who was comforting whom?

"You okay?" he asked softly. Rett tilted his head in confusion, and Noah watched in fascination as his eyebrows narrowed into a stern eleven.

"You were dreaming," Rett said, voice flat and succinct.

Noah chuckled, tugging on a feather, hoping Rett would take the hint and come a little closer. "I was. I'm awake now." He sucked in a breath when Rett reached forward to trace the scar running across his temple.

"Was it about this?"

Noah exhaled slowly and pulled Rett's hand from his face, holding it against his chest, the fingers lightly clasped inside his own. "Yeah."

Rett tugged his hand free and touched the scar again, eliciting a husky chuckle from Noah.

"Stubborn," he whispered.

Rett ignored him, fingertips learning the slick feel of the healed tissue, the jagged edges clearly delineated from the smooth surrounding skin, so frighteningly close to a beautiful eye. He followed its path to Noah's ear, lightly grazing the shell, the soft skin of the lobe, before he spoke. "I am sorry you no longer hear."

Noah found himself exhaling again, breath stuttering on a half laugh in its escape through his parted lips. "How did you know?"

Rett shrugged, the movement so small Noah might have missed it were the moon not casting the room with a faint silver glow. "I knew."

Noah felt a pinpoint of heat, deep behind his sternum, flushing outward until it reached his skin, enveloping him in a hazy blanket of warmth and desire. "I don't want to talk about it," he began hesitantly, returning his fingers to Rett's wing when he sensed the other man tense. "I was a soldier, once," he faltered and fell silent.

Rett looked at the silver tags and chain nestled in the center of Noah's chest; they glinted in the moonlight against skin he now knew the texture of, a smooth softness that was achingly familiar yet strange and new, and beckoned to him in a wave of yearning so pure it left him lightheaded. He heard the anxiety and regret behind Noah's quiet words and spread his wing until it covered the other man's lower body, inviting more touch.

Noah gave him a crooked grin. "You're just pacifying me now."

Rett shrugged again. "You like them. No one has," he looked away for a moment, into the shadows, the intensity of shared confessions unexpected and unfamiliar, raw. "No one has ever— If they give you comfort, they're yours."

Noah wet his lips, flustered and unsure of the meaning behind the loaded admission, the offer, *if it was an offer,* frustratingly unclear. He began to stroke the feathers again, boldly including the strength and tautness of Rett's tanned shoulder and the clenching muscles of his torso, as he continued his trek through the dark sheen.

He didn't miss the fine tremor in the wake of his touch and wished like hell Rett would lean over him again. The memory of Rett's full mouth so near his own made his blood pump hotter, faster.

"You should sleep," Rett murmured, withdrawing at last.

Noah caught his hand when he stood and the moment expanded, suspended in yet another layer of unexpected intimacy.

Noah squeezed his fingers. "You know," he said, fighting to keep his tone light, unwilling to break the strange spell that had woven around them, trapping them together in the dark glow of midnight. "At home, my crazy cat crawls into bed with me when I have a nightmare. She has, like, some sort of sixth sense. Any other time she spits and claws and avoids me like the plague."

Rett's eyes were unreadable as he gazed down at him. "Do you need me to stay?" he asked finally.

Noah's brow knitted together in a frown and he started to shake his head. He didn't *need* anyone.

"Move over," Rett said firmly, manhandling Noah to the opposite side of the bed before he could protest.

"Hey!" Noah objected, chuckling when a pillow hit him in the face. "Okay, you've had your fun. *Ow—*"

A wing slapped against his head before the bed dipped and a body, *Rett's body*, settled beside him.

When he tucked the errant pillow under his head and turned on his side, he found Rett's too-handsome face enticingly close, dark lashes fanning across a pale cheek when he blinked drowsily. Noah wondered fleetingly if they felt as silky as the feathers that lined the nape of his neck.

"This bed is too small for two people," Rett grumbled into the pale linens, shifting minutely closer, stretching one arm down at his side, then over his head, before grunting and throwing it across Noah's waist. He popped one eye open and Noah flushed, startled at being caught staring. "Sleep, Noah."

"Yeah, okay," Noah murmured, feeling warm and safe, burying his hands in feathers, a pleasant hum from the palm lying low across his hip anchoring him in the present, chasing away the remnants of the dream. His eyes fluttered closed and he let blackness overtake him.

GABRIEL WAITED at the base of the stairs until he no longer heard the murmur of voices above. When Rett didn't return, he smiled slowly and raised his gaze to the ornate chandelier overhead. He winked at the elaborate loops of gold and crystal. Things were most decidedly looking up.

The crystal twinkled in the moonlight, winking back.

CHAPTER 9

*N*oah stretched lazily, early morning sun streaming across the head of the bed, painting his face in golden light, preventing any hope he had of returning to sleep. His eyes popped open and he quickly turned his head; he was alone.

He sighed, scrubbing his face, trying desperately not to analyze the tightness in his belly. *Relief or frustration?* He sat up, studying the otherwise empty bed. If he didn't know better, he would never guess a strange winged man had slept nestled into his side.

His gut tightened further and his groin answered with a hot spurt of undeniable desire. "Yeah, okay, not relief," he muttered, throwing off the sheet, glancing backward as he left the bed, a millisecond after swearing to himself he wouldn't look.

Not even a single damn feather.

Noah knew he should retrace his steps the second he heard the tell-tale patter of water falling on tile, a clear indication the shower was otherwise occupied.

He *should* have.

But he didn't.

He stood in what he now knew to be Rett's bedroom, squirming with the deluge of too graphic images and impure thoughts, bolstered by a faint memory of warm skin and slick feathers, and possibly a knee wedged firmly between his thighs.

"*Mother of Christ,*" he swore, trying in vain not to stare at the massive bed under the windows. Bigger than a king and stretching for metaphorical miles across the room, he had an immediate and vivid understanding of why Rett had complained about the size of Noah's bed.

A body, or two, could stretch out, roll around, get...*ambitious,* on a bed that size.

Noah swallowed and he apologized silently to his dick, which was feeling pretty damn neglected and long-suffering, having been subjected to a botched attempt at relief the night before, when Noah had fallen sleep mid-process, pre-nightmare.

Noah came to his senses, hit with an undeniably stark clarity that Rett was, right this second, standing under streams of falling water in his massive shower, which probably rivaled his massive bed in scope, *naked,* wet, dark wings probably trailing behind him in a shining path of droplets and suds and *nopenopenope.* Noah most definitely could not deal. He turned to flee, brought up short by the bath door opening, revealing an equally startled (and magnificently naked) Rett.

"Fuck," Noah breathed. He slammed his eyes closed, then covered them with a palm, for good measure. "Sorry! Sorry, I'll just—"

"Do you wish to use the shower?" Rett asked calmly.

Noah heard the rustle of footsteps and felt the air move gently beside him. Or maybe that was that goddamn proximity beacon he had developed that pinged like a siren whenever Rett was in the same room. The fucker was *standing right beside him. Naked.*

"Nope, I'm good," Noah said.

"I've covered myself with a towel, Noah." Rett's voice was amused. "You can lower your hand."

I'm not sure that's any better, Noah thought resentfully, his fucked up, supercharged imagination firing images of *nearly* naked Rett wrapped in a tiny white towel, dark trail of hair down the center of his belly disappearing into—

"Noah?"

"Yeah?" Noah squeaked.

"The water is nicely warm."

And Goddamn it, Noah realized then that Rett fucking *knew* what he was doing, with that gravelly tone and freshly shampooed smell and blazing heat coming off his damp skin in waves so strong it knocked all of Noah's senses for a loop. He lowered his hand, steeling himself for his first (*second*) glance. "Maybe I do want to take a shower," he said, childishly proud of his steady tone.

That fucking towel was tiny.

Rett's lower lip was twisted between neat, white teeth, hiding a smile, and it pissed him off. "You have another towel, or should we share?" Noah asked boldly. *Two can play that game, asshole.* When Rett's hand immediately tugged on the white knot at his waist, Noah panicked and grabbed his wrist. "Wait! I was kidding!" He said in a rush.

Rett chuckled and the deep rumble made Noah's stomach topple over in a lazy somersault. "There are towels outside the shower door, on a shelf." Rett turned away and began to rummage through a chest of drawers.

Noah shook his hand, fingers tingling from their too-brief brush with a smooth, damp arm. He cleared his throat. "I don't suppose you have a pair of jeans in that drawer, do you?" When Rett threw him a questioning look, he grinned unsteadily. "Gabe is doing my laundry."

When Rett's hand hovered over a pair of dark linen pants, Noah grunted. "And none of those funny pants you wear, either."

Rett straightened, slamming the drawer with a thud. "Gabriel, whose father was a well-respected tailor, constructed my clothing," he said stiffly.

"Yeah, okay," Noah said soothingly, grinning at the wriggly movements of Rett's pissed off feathers. For a man who had been damned for centuries, a horror-novel villain in the flesh, he was pretty cute when he was mad. "They look really nice on you," he offered.

Rett snorted.

"But I prefer all-American blue denim, if you got any."

A few moments later, Rett handed him a pair of creased, never-worn jeans and an equally stiff t-shirt with a county fair logo blazoned across the front.

"Gabriel is swayed by the shops in town," he offered at Noah's puzzled frown.

"Ah. No underwear?" Noah teased. "Guess I'm going commando, then."

This was met with a blank expression.

Noah coughed self-consciously, his own obvious state of undress, *their* obvious state of undresss, *together,* burning at the tips of his ears, heat flooding his cheeks. "Nevermind." He turned and made his escape in a few quick strides. He was pretty sure he could hear Rett laughing as he firmly closed the bathroom door.

Feathery asshole, he thought, leaning on the paneled hardwood and breathing deep.

Noah didn't know what he had envisioned when Gabe had first mentioned Rett's giant shower, but it wasn't the glass-encased room within a room he found inside the bath. It was, for lack of a better word, magnificent.

He circled the three glass walls slowly, blowing out an appreciative whistle. Tiled floor to ceiling in pale, iridescent blue, in a twelve by ten foot space, the expanded shower featured multiple showerheads, bench seating and incorporated windows original to the house.

"This must have taken them years to finish," he murmured, shedding his boxers and clicking open the fogged glass door. Inside, it was even prettier, tranquil. The steam had dissipated from Rett's shower, but a hot dampness remained, along with an elusive whiff of fragrant masculinity, the same as which had been haunting Noah for days.

He adjusted the water and turned on the crisscrossing heads, sighing in relief as the hot stream deluged him from all sides.

He tried not to think of the previous inhabitant.

Standing in the same spot.

Naked.

Wet.

Damn it.

Eight minutes later his legs were trembling and his skin was flushed, but the pleasant aftereffect of lingering orgasm was a nice buffer for the water that sluiced over his body. His blessedly clear and relaxed brain skittered over musings of whether Rett had entertained thoughts of *Noah* in the shower this morning too.

He raked his palm across his mouth and chased that heady notion right down the drain, blinking the water from his lashes.

He opened the various bottles and sniffed, searching for *the one* without success. He grinned at the wide assortment; it would seem Rett may have a bath product fetish, and that was the kind of information Noah was happy to squirrel away for future ammunition. He tried in vain not to imagine how each individual gel or lotion would smell mixed with Rett's own unique scent, succeeding in driving himself mildly crazy and pitifully aroused again before he settled on a generic shampoo and body wash. He finished his morning routine efficiently, if not in any particular hurry. The rumble of his stomach urged him from the glass room more than the pull of the house's other occupant.

Or so he told himself.

Downstairs, he frowned to find he was alone in the house, a covered dish of bacon and scrambled eggs accompanied by a hot carafe of coffee and a single place setting at the kitchen table. He ate, fidgety and uneasy in the silence, wishing there were a radio or television or *something* to distract him from the vast nothingness of the massive house. There were times the mansion was almost comfortingly alive with the warmth of remembered family and friendship; but then there were times like this, when it seemed empty and dead, a tomb that beat an oppressive desire for Noah to leave.

He shivered and admonished his overactive imagination. "You're on a roll, today," he muttered.

After he rinsed his plate and cup, he ventured out back with his box of hardware store purchases, waving at Gabriel in the chicken coop across the yard. He crouched beside the Road Runner and sorted the items by type and use. When he found the green and yellow container of rose food at the bottom of the box, he stared at the garden thoughtfully, before ambling back into the kitchen in search of a pitcher.

~

RETT FLEW LOW, just clearing the uppermost branches of cypress bordering the property line of Rosewood, ignoring the itch between his shoulder blades that told him *too far, go back!* He needed distance and speed today.

He had cooked breakfast for Noah before he fled; Noah who had slept curled onto his side, cheek pillowed on a fist, mouth open with soft snores. Noah who had clutched tightly to Rett's waist when another dream had gripped him in the night, then melted into his chest, nuzzling his neck, mouth pressing open and hot along his collar bone in a silent thank you as Rett had rubbed soothing circles on his back.

Noah who this morning clearly had no memory of the second dream or its aftermath.

Rett circled the house, frowning as he recognized the former soldier at the edge of the roses, a pitcher in hand.

~

NOAH JUMPED when Rett dropped out of nowhere beside him as he crouched to pour the blue liquid around the base of the first rose bush. "What the he—"

Rett knocked the pitcher from his hands, upending it, the contents splashing over Noah's head, soaking his shirt.

Noah sputtered, spitting the foul taste from his mouth. "God damn it, Rett, what's got into you?" He scraped furiously at his eyes.

"What are you doing to my daughter's rose?" Rett growled, eyes dark and fuming.

Noah clambered to his feet, still spitting, anger flaming bright.

"Fuck, Rett, what's the matter with you! I don't know what the hell's in that stuff! I'll probably get cancer, according to the state of California." He kicked the pitcher aside and stalked across the yard toward the Road Runner.

Rett gaped after him, mouth working, fury leaving him in a quiet rush of confused affection. He had understood Noah's individual words, but not a whit of their meaning. He flew to beat him to Gabriel's door, but Noah ignored his quiet, "Noah," before disappearing into Gabe's living room.

He reappeared a moment later unrolling a green hose, the end kinked in one hand, water dripping from the nozzle. He ripped his t-shirt over his head with his free hand and unkinked the hose, gasping when the well water hit his overheated skin.

Rett stared. "Noah," he tried again.

"Shut up, Rett," Noah said around a mouthful of water before he spat in the yard. He bent at the waist and thoroughly wet his hair, scrubbing it with his hands to remove all of the plant food. When he stood, he flung his head back and doused his chest and back again, goosebumps peppering his skin. He could practically *feel* his lips turning blue and he knew his nipples were hard as a rock. And if that *fucker* was looking…he chanced a glance for confirmation. Rett was most definitely looking.

He turned the hose on him, covering Rett from head to toe in one wide swath of ice-cold spray.

Rett blinked and then grabbed the hose from Noah's hands in a flash.

Noah swallowed his grin, anger gone as quickly as it had flared. "You're all wet."

Rett hit him in the face with the full power of the hose.

"Rett!" Noah sputtered, laughing and ducking, charging the other man at waist level with all his weight. They both toppled backward onto the ground, Rett's deep grunt giving Noah pause as he lay on top of him. "Oh shit, did I hurt your wings?"

Rett flipped them, Noah's breath knocked out in a *whoosh*, when he landed flat on his back. "They're fine," Rett smirked, flapping them overhead and spraying water in a wide pattern over the grass.

"Show off," Noah complained, wiggling. Rett had him firmly pinned beneath him and he still held the water hose, absently letting the flow hit Noah square in the chest.

"That's cold, asshole," Noah pointed out, trying to free an arm to prepare for defensive maneuvers.

Rett's eyes followed the water's clear trail, shifting to hard dusky nubs.

Noah squirmed again, embarrassingly interested in the spark of fascination he could read in Rett's eyes, acutely aware that if Rett moved his thigh even three inches to the left, there would be yet another revelation in the arousal attributes of one Noah Hix. "You wanna let me up now?"

Rett refocused on his mouth and for one breathtaking moment, Noah thought, *This is it.* His tongue darted out, wetting his lips in unconscious invitation.

"What are you two doing?" Gabriel asked, his silhouette blocking the sun as his shadow fell over them. "You're going to run the well dry." He pulled the hose from Rett's hand and kinked it before disappearing into the little house.

Noah lay frozen and still, caught in Rett's unblinking stare for a long beat before Rett sat back and rolled gracefully to his feet. He held out a hand and Noah accepted it.

Noah shook off the remaining water, frantically trying to remember what it was he had meant to say before they had ventured markedly off track. His body had apparently missed the whole *sexy playtime's over* memo, and he resisted the urge to cross his arms over his too pert chest.

Rett's expression was faraway as he turned toward the garden. "I didn't mean to spill the liquid on you," he offered quietly. "What was it?"

Noah flinched when Rett turned that intense blue gaze on him. His lips parted in a wistful smile, and he wondered how many times in his life a single moment represented a fork in a road, and he had taken the wrong path. "Rose food. I bought it at the hardware store, but I didn't want to get your hopes up. Thought I'd give it a whirl first, before you got home."

Rett tried not to react, but Noah saw something flicker in his eyes before he hid it. Heat, possession, and something else, something that unfurled inside Noah's belly, that long tendril of electricity that seemed to snap to life between them whenever they were together.

"Thank you," Rett said roughly, his deep rumble warming Noah from the inside out.

"I, uh, don't suppose you want to try again?" Noah grinned.

Rett cocked his head. "Try what, exactly," he asked slowly, and that tendril in Noah's gut exploded into a thousand volts of lightening dancing between them.

"The food," Noah said, breath too fast, heart racing. "The roses." He took a well-intentioned step backward and then another, and then started across the lawn to fetch the discarded pitcher. "You should go find some dry clothes," he called over his shoulder.

He blinked when he looked up to find Rett standing at the rose bush, holding the pitcher on the crook of one finger.

"You are a coward, Noah Hix," Rett said, before shooting into the sky, his path this time obscured by the sun when Noah tried to follow him with his eyes.

CHAPTER 10

*R*ett was watching him.

Every instinct in Noah's body was honed to it, a restless anticipation alerting him to the distant glances trailing down his back, his hips, his arms. He pursed his lips and yanked a corroded plug free from the housing under the hood of the car, dropping it at his feet where it bounced under the tire, nestled away in celadon weeds.

He was hot, hungry, tired, and covered in a satisfying smear of grease and sweat.

And he *wanted.*

"YOU COULD PROPOSE YOUR HELP, instead of skulking in the window," Gabe offered drily.

Rett stiffened. "I am not *skulking.* I'm merely observing in case our friend Earl makes a reappearance."

"Why do you insist on naming those vile creatures?" Gabe asked. He moaned in obscene approval as he scooped up the last bite of pie on his fork. "This pie is amazing."

"Noah is going to be very disappointed in you," Rett murmured, shifting to the left when the man below them moved from of his immediate line of sight.

"I'm counting on you to distract him," Gabe replied cheerfully, fork clattering on the saucer when he set both down on an empty tread.

Rett blinked at him in confusion. "Excuse me?"

Gabe rolled his eyes. "Use your handsome face for something other than a scowl?" He suggested. "Flutter those damnable wings? He's clearly enamored of them." *And you,* Gabe thought.

"I haven't the slightest idea as to what you are referring," Rett sniffed, fighting a telltale blush. "Or what games you seem intent on playing," he added pointedly.

"Yes, you do," Gabe crowed. "You like him, admit it."

"I will not." But Rett was smiling now, Gabriel's jubilant disposition contagious. He took the stairs slowly. "What's gotten into you anyway?"

"Oh nothing," Gabe said airily. "Just feeling optimistic for the first time in a about a century and a half."

"Funny."

"You should cook dinner for him."

"What?" Rett's eyebrows shot into his hairline. "I can't cook."

"You handled breakfast all right."

"Scrambling an egg is not exactly culinary savoir faire," Rett said with a wry smile.

Gabe rubbed his palms together. "No, no, it's perfect. I'll help you with dinner, and the two of you can have a nice, quiet evening." He wiggled his eyebrows. "I'll make myself scarce."

Rett's gaze was calculating. "Are you matchmaking, Father Gabriel?" He shook his head. "Even it weren't for the obvious species discrepancies," he fluttered one wing, "you might have noticed that Noah is male."

"Rett," Gabe soothed, reaching for his friend's biceps and giving them a hard squeeze. "Get thee with the twenty-first century."

Rett barked a laugh. "Your television box has warped you, my good man. Need I remind you of the little towns called—"

"Don't you dare quote Genesis to me, Everett Blackburn," Gabe warned with more than a little bite. He squeezed his arms again. "He likes you, too. Trust me."

Rett stared at a smudge on the fading wallpaper. "Do you still have the dress clothes you were attempting to alter?" he finally asked, head angling toward door.

Gabe swallowed back a grin, shocked that it had really been that simple. "I do. I'll fetch them now along with a chicken I was preparing to roast." He spun in a lively twirl as he danced across the foyer, pausing when Rett made no move to follow him. "Rett?"

Rett's gaze was still trained on the wall, faraway look in his eyes. "Do you think of that night? When Charlotte took Emmeline and left on the boat?"

"Rett," Gabe repeated his name, no more than a sigh, throat tight with emotions that should by all rights have long since faded, dispersed into a murky past.

"I think of her face," Rett continued softly. "Her eyes, so like mine, and I wonder what became of her. If she still called for me in the night when she had nightmares." He pinned Gabe in place with a hard glare, eyes dark, his handsome face drawn and troubled. "If I was the nightmare she saw in her dreams."

"You weren't," Gabe said gently. "I believe that she remembered you as you were, before." He trailed off, because no words would give respite from the fate Rett had endured. He had lost more than his humanity or his way of life; he had lost the last hold on his heart by the cruelest possible means, wrenched from his hands in the dead of the night.

They were both aware there was no way to know what terrors had lived on in young Emmeline's nightmares.

She had never been seen by either of them again.

Noah carefully closed the kitchen door behind him, waiting silent and still before crossing to the sink to wash the grime from under his fingernails. He scrubbed the bar of soap into a thick lather, working it into his knuckles and palms, the knob of his wrist, the length of his forearms.

It wasn't as though he was avoiding Rett, he argued with himself, as he rinsed and lathered again.

He was merely being politely quiet, so as not to disturb him. He could be resting.

He watched the last of the soap bubbles whorl down the drain.

"Are you hungry?"

Noah jumped. "Christ."

"Sorry," Rett said. "I thought you heard me."

"I didn't." Noah tossed the smudged and dampened towel over the side of the sink, not looking at the man he could feel hovering just outside of his peripheral vision. He felt more than saw him retreat at Noah's unspoken dismissal, fading into the pantry, trying to disappear into the depths of the house. "Yes, I'm hungry," he called.

He waited, cursing the unsteadiness of his pulse and the anxious need for Rett to come back. A soft rustle in the doorway settled the rapid beat of his heart. "Sandwich?" He asked calmly, standing inside the refrigerator door, exhaling silently through his nose.

"Okay," Rett replied, hesitating by the table. "Noah?"

"Hmm?" Noah set out cold sliced ham and pickles and mustard, reaching for the loaf of bread wrapped tightly in wax paper in a quaint wooden box. He shuffled through a drawer for a knife.

"I," Rett cleared his throat and pulled at a chair, the legs scraping noisily across the floor, infringing on the quiet hush of the kitchen. "I thought I would prepare dinner." He bit his lip when Noah continued to spread mustard on a slice of bread in slow strokes. "Roast chicken." The words tapered off until there was only the sound of the too patient knife.

Noah carefully aligned the crusts of the bread, then sliced the sandwiches in equal diagonal halves. He placed the neat triangles on two pale blue saucers and rinsed the knife under the faucet before turning at last.

"I like chicken." His eyes met Rett's, found the blue clouded and uncertain, and the mirrored anxiety served to quell his own nerves.

He was still overheated, skin stretched too thin, but he brought the plates to the table and sat dow across from the man he no longer thought of as a creature, embracing a fresh thrill of anticipation before he took his first bite. "I like chicken a lot," he winked, emulating a casualness he didn't feel, swan diving into the unknown at the bottom of this cliff.

Rett gingerly picked up one half of his sandwich, mouth suspiciously tilted at one corner. "I thought as much."

They ate ham and mustard on homemade bread and smiled over glasses of iced tea and Noah thought he might need to let the car dry out another day before beginning to work on her in earnest.

<h1 style="text-align:center">CHAPTER 11</h1>

The air stirred, hot and humid, when Rett's feet first met the gravel of the road, and then Noah's a split second after. His hands slipped from Noah's hips, more reluctantly than he expected, and he stepped back. "Take care on your walk."

Noah caught himself before his body swayed in the direction of Rett's retreat. He wondered if he would always suffer the same dip and shudder of his stomach when Rett lifted him from the ground. At least he had kept his eyes open this time.

Mostly.

He cleared his throat. "Thanks, Rett. I'll be back as soon as I grab some more supplies. I need a way to call home, and I forgot yesterday," he stopped abruptly, self-conscious and rambling. Rett wouldn't grasp the concept of a cell phone, and why was he explaining himself, anyway?

"I understand," Rett said solemnly. "You should quell their fears. There is no cause to worry them needlessly."

Noah laughed softly, the nervous tension that Rett's proximity inevitably caused bleeding away with the man's odd formality and serious expression. "Rett, no one talks like that. At least, not anymore." Rett studied him so seriously, Noah flushed and ducked his head.

"What should I say?" Rett asked.

Noah licked his lips, pulse fluttering madly again. "Nevermind. You're doing just fine. I'll be back as soon as I can."

Rett nodded, taking another step toward the safety of the trees. "Be safe," he said again.

Noah gave a little wave, ending in a delayed jab of his index finger. "And no squash!"

He was rewarded with the ring of Rett's laughter as he took to the sky.

IT SHOULDN'T HAVE SURPRISED Noah when a stranger on their streets, twice in the same number of days, drew attention. Men tipped their heads in greeting when he passed and pretty girls smiled, eyes coy and coquettish.

He nodded when prompted, polite smiles, his usual harmless flirtations conspicuously lacking in appeal today. He was glad to leave the sidewalk when he reached the diner, bell jingling cheerfully overhead as he pushed through the door.

"Well, if it isn't our handsome traveler," the redhead from the day before exclaimed with a smile. "How did we get so lucky?"

"It was the pie," Noah winked, waving at Benny through the kitchen window. "Think you could fix me up a few more slices?"

"Different specials today," Maisy said, nodding toward the cake stands.

One of the glass-covered dishes held the most beautiful pie Noah had ever seen; his mouth watered at the height of the meringue. "Lemon," he said pleadingly.

Benny snorted, wrists crossed on the sill of the cutout in the wall. "You're a lost cause, soldier."

"I'm a slave to pastry," Noah grinned. "And the fruit?"

"That's blueberry," Maisy offered, already slicing two fat pieces of lemon meringue and wedging them into a cardboard cake box.

Noah sighed happily. "Better make it three of each." Rett had confessed earlier that Gabe had eaten the slices of pecan resting in the fridge, and while Noah *should* skip the fucker for eating the last slice of pie, he technically still owed the former priest for saving his life.

"You're not gonna fit behind the steering wheel of that fancy car, if you're not careful," Benny warned, slipping through with the next swing of the kitchen door. He slung a towel over his shoulder and leaned on the counter. "You have lunch?"

"I did," Noah nodded, mouth watering as fat, juicy blueberries fell off the side of Maisy's knife. "And shut up," he added, smile wide and relaxed.

"How goes the repairs?" Benny poured two cups of coffee and slid one in front of Noah.

"Slow," Noah grimaced. "This morning I drained everything and pulled all the plugs. I'm countin' on that pie to wash the taste of gas from my mouth."

Benny arched one eyebrow. "You better be careful, nearest ambulance service is a good hour away. You get unleaded in your belly and you're as good as dead."

"Nah, I've been siphoning since I was a delinquent." Noah shrugged. "Not my most prized skill, but it sure as hell came in handy today."

They sipped their coffee companionably while Maisy tied a piece of cream twine around the cardboard box.

"Here you go, stranger. I'll let the boss ring you up. I'm takin' my break."

"Break?" Benny asked incredulously, watching the redhead's hips sashay away. He turned back to Noah with a smirk. "I like that. You're the first soul we've seen since lunch. *Break,*" he scoffed into his mug.

Noah chuckled. "The trials of the small business owner, huh?"

"Good help is hard to find," Benny agreed with a grin. "So Noah, what do you do in Kansas?"

The previous day they had uncovered brief tidbits of shared history in between the meatloaf special and the locals who dropped in for coffee and pie. Noah was former Army, Benny had been in the Navy. Although he was mindful of protecting Rett and Gabe, Noah had seen no reason why he couldn't be truthful about his own back-ground. And Benny's slow-drawling grin was contagious.

"Mechanic, mostly," he offered, blowing on the top layer of dark liquid in his mug.

"You still a delinquent?" Benny winked.

Noah's laugh was quick and unfettered, and he shook his head in amusement. "Nope, totally respectable now. Unfortunately."

Benny looked up when the bell over the door rang out. "You on foot again, brother? I could give you a ride. I've got an errand to run out past that old haunt of yours."

Noah stared, mug halfway to his lips.

Benny lightly pounded a closed fist on the counter, his voice low and soothing to ward off Noah's uneasy expression. "Chip Rodriguez passed you walking on Parish Road 1105 yesterday. Not many options out thataway."

Noah grunted and took a sip. "Small towns."

"You got it," Benny saluted and ambled down the counter to wait on his new customer.

GABE MUMBLED under his breath as Rett twitched, tense and uneasy. "Hold still," he said around the straight pin between his lips.

"Then hurry up," Rett spat. Although he had the grace to look contrite a few seconds later. "My apologies." He remained motionless as Gabe pinned the white dress shirt in place for stitching.

Gabe had removed twin portions of the shirt's back, cleverly rehemming the openings to allow space for Rett's wings, before tailoring a dark blue waistcoat with a similar alteration. He adjusted the new fastenings at Rett's waist and tied off the last knot before stepping back in satisfaction.

"All finished," he said with a flourish. He reached up to brush a tuft of dark down from Rett's starched collar. "Fine work, if I might be so arrogant."

Rett grimaced. "I look ridiculous."

"Actually, you look quite debonair," Gabe offered, eyes twinkling.

"Shouldn't you be discouraging this, *Father*?"

Rett wouldn't meet his gaze but Gabe understood his meaning and shrugged. "I care little for bigotry and judgmental musings, Rett," he said quietly, straightening the waistcoat with a sharp tug. He smiled. "You, of all people, should know that."

"This is insanity," Rett grumbled, but from the way he gingerly touched the cuff at his wrist, and smoothed his palm down the buttoned-front of the vest, Gabe knew his friend was secretly pleased.

"Love is a temporary insanity," Gabe quoted softly.

Rett huffed, cheeks flushing warmly. "Don't impose unnecessary sentiment, Gabriel. You always were an incurable romantic." The words were intended to be derisive, but his delivery was lacking, soft. His heart began to thrum underneath the silk vest as he wondered what Noah's reaction might be when he saw him.

"Tis true, tis true," Gabe mock swooned. "There once was a boy from Nantucket—"

"Gabe!" Rett broke in with a choked laugh.

Gabe chuckled and clapped a hand to Rett's shoulder. "Now let's go see about your chicken."

NOAH WATCHED Benny argue with a young woman on a rundown porch, an unkempt toddler clinging to her faded housedress as it fluttered around her bare calves. Even through the windshield, he could see a fresh bruise blossoming along the side of her face. She was shaking her head violently, arms crossed in front of her body in a lonely embrace, as Benny's hands cupped her jaw.

Noah looked away from the intimate moment, studying the waving grasses of the unplowed fields surrounding the old house. He glanced up in surprised when the driver's door opened and Benny slid behind the wheel.

"Stubborn woman," Benny muttered slamming the truck into gear. His jaw was unyielding, cheeks ruddy with emotion.

"Friend in trouble?" Noah asked casually, although he recognized when anger's origin came from a deeper place.

"You could say that." Benny backed the truck up, and turned right down the old gravel road, the few miles to Rosewood now noticeably brief.

As they passed, Noah watched the woman bury her face in her hands before she bent and picked up the baby and went back into the sad little house. "I've got time," he said, setting the pie on the seat beside him. "You keep that cooler back there stocked?" He jerked his head toward the bed of the pickup, where an ice chest and a tackle box lay beside several fishing poles.

Benny chuckled softly. "Always. You feel up to some giggin'? I hear the crawfish are thick after the storm."

"I can honestly say I have no earthly idea what you're talking about, but if it involves craw*dads*, I'm all in."

"Crawdads? Pshaw," Benny scoffed, slowing and turning the truck around in the middle of the dirt road. "Brother, hang onto your shorts. I'm going to do something about your alarming lack of Cajun education."

Noah clasped Benny's hand through the driver's window, the night so deep and black it swallowed up the truck's headlights, insulating them on the barren country road. "You stay away from farmhouses and angry husbands and go straight home, you hear?"

Benny laughed softly. "Yeah, I hear. You sure you don't want some of our catch?"

"Nah, you keep 'em. Make somethin' fancy for tomorrow's special," Noah winked. He hesitated, the story of the woman on the porch fresh and painful and making him uneasily homesick. "You gonna be all right?"

"You don't always get to choose, Noah," Benny said with a sad smile, crickets and cicadas filling the air with their night song. "Sometimes your heart chooses for you."

Noah nodded. He thought he might be beginning to understand that.

"How the hell you gettin' across that again?" Benny asked incredulously, deftly changing the subject as he peered at the muddy trail disappearing into the bayou.

Noah waved off his concern, saying a prayer that Rett was safely tucked away, deep within the mansion. "There's a couple of logs, just down the way there." He pointed in a vague southerly direction. "I'll get across." He stepped back from the open window. "Thanks for the lift."

Benny's eyes were trained on the shadowy shapes of the cypress, his expression thoughtful. "I always did want to get a look inside this old place." He glanced at Noah with a grin. "Is it really haunted?"

Noah laughed easily, hoping the nervous tic along his left cheekbone was invisible in the dim night. "Not that I can tell. But I'll keep you posted." He slapped the door. "You drive careful."

Benny nodded, his gaze still tracing the outline of the house through the trees. "Yeah." He eased the gearshift into reverse. "You don't eat all that pie at once, Hix. Remember what I said: ain't no ambulance comin' to get you if you overindulge yourself into a sugar coma."

"Har har," Noah grinned. He waved, exhaling in relief when the truck finally began to move, waiting in the road until it was gone, twin pricks of glowing red in the distance, before he started down the sloping grasses of the ditch toward the bayou.

He stumbled backward with a surprised grunt when a figure loomed large and imposing, appearing suddenly in his path and knocking the cake box from his hands. "Fuck, Rett," he breathed after the initial shock, barely resisting the urge to clutch at his chest. "What the hell, man? You scared me half the death."

"What have you done?" Rett growled, advancing on him again, eyes black with fury, wings poised menacingly over Noah's head.

Noah stumbled again, scrambling for purchase on the dew-slick grass. "What do you mean, what have I done? I—"

His words were cut off when Rett grabbed him around the waist and shot into the air and over the trees in a heartstopping rush of wind and gravity. Noah's stomach bottomed out and he fell, hitting hard on the mossy earth when Rett released him on the other side of the water. He coughed, wheezing for air as he rolled to his knees, his knuckles scraped raw where they dragged tree roots and gravel.

Rett didn't afford him the option of explanation, yanking him to his feet by two fistfuls of shirt. He pulled Noah's face close to his own. "Who was he? What did you tell him?"

Noah gripped Rett's wrists, reeling and off-balance, lightheaded, scrambling mentally to catch up. His hip ached from his tumble across the ground, and his pride was starting to burn, engulfed quickly by a hot flare of anger. "You need to calm the fuck down," he said quietly, meeting Rett's snapping eyes with a cool, green gaze.

Just as quickly as he had appeared, Rett was gone, and Noah lurched when his shirt was released as the creature took to the air.

"Rett!" he yelled, confusion and rage warring at the back of his throat. "Get your feathery ass down here, you coward!" He volleyed Rett's earlier accusation into the night in a cheap parting shot, but the sky remained still and dark, empty of stars or moon or beast.

CHAPTER 12

The fanlight and sidelight windows of the surround rattled when Noah kicked the door closed behind him. He took the steps of the curving staircase two at a time, propelled equally by a biting irritation and an unfamiliar angst, but a noise from the back of the house had him quickly reversing direction. He stalked across the formal marble entry, and through the dark pantry, before he was caught up short in the kitchen doorway by a figure at the sink.

Glossy wings brushed the floor, dejected, black feather tips stark against the the pale wood. In his hands Rett cradled a dented and forlorn cardboard container.

An unexpected flicker of emotion wound through Noah's bones at the sight of that damned pink box as he fought valiantly to cling to his anger.

"I'm sorry," Rett said with quiet composure, setting the box carefully in the deep porcelain basin of the sink, effectively slicing the beginning and the end from Noah's unspoken tirade with an unhurried grace. "I don't know why I was so... angry."

Noah stared, crippled by the gentleness of Rett's fingers as he worked the knots in the dirty twine.

"Your pie is?" Rett tilted his head, studying the contents of the box after he opened the lid. "Flat?" He lifted the package with both hands and turned toward Noah, presenting a carefully empty expression alongside the sodden disaster of pastry and fruit.

Noah liked to think his senses had been uniquely honed by his years as a soldier and the loss of his hearing, but nothing in his war-torn life had prepared him for the crushing awareness that seized him in that moment. The disordered jumble of meringue and blueberries was painfully inferior to a starched white collar against a beautifully tanned throat, or a midnight hued waistcoat echoing the blue of Rett's eyes. His heart knocking harshly against the cage of his ribs, Noah knew with startling clarity that something seismic was shifting within him, and he would never be the same.

He scrambled to recover, disquieted and confused by an uncharacteristic desire to express himself verbally. He hadn't missed the way Rett had become similarly immobilized, probably by Noah's unresponsiveness, and he tried to salvage the moment, lest Rett turn away and they lose this...*whatever* they had become.

"What the hell are you wearing?" Noah asked dumbly, instantly disappointed by his predictable failure to connect his mouth to his brainstem, although maybe the words weren't important so long as they kept Rett from running away. But—*damn it*—Noah wished those words hadn't been his first. He exhaled slowly, pensively turning over new ones in his head, rubbing his jaw and wincing at the burning reminder of his cracked and bloodied hand.

"You're hurt." Rett's face fell further, his mouth a grim line of distress, and he set the box on the counter. "Come here." He turned on the tap, fingertips under the stream, assessing the temperature.

Normally Noah might have bristled at the commanding tone, but he was pitifully thankful for any excuse that brought his aching, greedy body within touching distance of the man at the sink. "It's nothing," he said gruffly, keeping a few sanity preserving inches between them as he shoved his hands under the faucet. His pulse skipped a beat when a white-clad arm reached across him for a bar of homemade soap, and he pulled back with a frown, ignoring his body's protest at the retreat. "That's going to sting like a bitch."

"Don't be such a baby," Rett murmured, catching Noah's wrists to keep him close.

Noah's brain stalled at the first touch and then ceased functioning entirely when long, elegant fingers worked creamy suds into the cuts and abrasions, tenderly cleansing dirt and debris from the shallow wounds. Rett angled Noah's hand into the water at regular intervals to rinse, and then repeated the process all over again. When he seemed satisfied that both hands were clean, he held Noah's battered knuckles lightly in his palm.

Noah had become grounded during the procedure, watching those beautiful hands care for the wounds they had wrought, the alien white cuff now damp with water and the residue of soap. Rett's handsome face was so temptingly close that Noah allowed himself the unchecked luxury of studying the sharp cut of his jaw and the shapely curve of his mouth. He liked the way Rett's dark lashes blinked slow and unhurried, a thick shadow that masked a bright, clear blue. He smiled when the color turned stormy at a particularly stubborn bit of dirt, as if the stain was a personal affront.

Suddenly Noah couldn't remember why he had been so angry.

When Rett leaned away for a strip of soft, white terrycloth, Noah had had enough. Enough of the tight band across his chest and the butterflies heaving acid in his stomach; enough fighting the hunger that boiled in his blood and tied his tongue up in knots. When it seemed as though Rett's palm might slip away entirely, Noah tightened his grasp and tugged, using inertia where words once again failed him, and pressed their lips together in a swift, closed-mouth kiss.

Rett froze.

Noah flushed, cursing his recklessness and his inability to accurately read people or situations. He squeezed his eyes tight as he pulled away, memorizing the cling of their lips, the skin tacky and soft as they slid apart, because despite his mortification, he never wanted to forget.

But then Rett was digging his fingers into the back of his scalp and kissing him back, mouth opening hot and wet and desperate, moaning as he scrabbled at the short strands of Noah's crown to anchor him in place, as though he might disappear.

As if there as anywhere else Noah wanted to be.

They kissed, standing at the sink, perfect, wet passes of lips and tongue, and Noah thought he might actually die if Rett stopped touching him. He shifted them, pressing Rett more firmly into the counter and a wing knocked a glass to the floor, where it shattered into a million glittering shards. Noah grunted in apology but Rett held him fast; there were mouths learning the taste of one another, and broken, whispered words to swallow and absorb, and the glass could wait, it would keep.

Noah dug his fingers into Rett's hips, memorizing the curves of the bones with a singular guided devotion. If he had given this any forethought at all, he might have been inclined to take things slow, but Rett was steamrolling past all of Noah's secret midnight musings, chasing the mewling gasps that fell embarrassingly from Noah's lips, as though he had nothing better to do with the rest of his life than to force the sounds to the surface and then drink them down, again and again.

Noah bucked in surprise when Rett's hands worked their way under the hem of his t-shirt.

"You smell like fish," Rett muttered unexpectedly, and it made Noah laugh, the sound breaking on an quick inhale when Rett's fingers raked down his sides.

"You smell like *you*," Noah groaned in reply, finally finding his voice but abandoning it in favor of breathing, and for burying his nose behind Rett's ear, fighting an urge to just grind and grind against him.

Rett chuckled darkly and slid his hands down to squeeze Noah's hips. "I don't know what that means." He dipped his head, to lick at the pulse point on Noah's throat, and Noah gasped, dragging Rett's head up by a handful of dark curls.

"You're killing me," Noah ground out between his teeth before he crashed their mouths together again.

Another flutter, and another glass, and then Rett was laughing against him, the sound deep and sweet and sexy.

Noah had no idea how he had gone from scrabbling for control to losing it again in the space of a heartbeat. "Rett," he sighed, settling his hips into a rhythm, deciding friction might be the answer to this new and very real fear of spontaneous combustion.

Rett eagerly matched each movement and Noah knew it was dangerous, this teetering on the edge, but it felt too good to stop and they sucked at the damp air between their mouths, lips rubbing, hips shifting in tandem. Rett dragged the hem of Noah's shirt higher until Noah lifted his arms to allow him to pull it over his head. For a beat there was only silence, and Rett paused, eyes hot, before dropping a gentle, open-mouthed kiss to Noah's bare shoulder.

Noah cupped his jaw, stilling them both, and Rett froze, eyes blown dark with desire but shuttering swiftly in the face of Noah's hesitation. Noah brushed the hair from his forehead and kissed him lightly. "I want to look at you," he reassured him, voice low, their mouths brushing with the movement of each word as it left his lips.

Rett shuddered as his eyes fell closed.

Noah kissed each eyelid, then rubbed his lips along the bolt of his jaw. "What are you wearing?" He asked again, but this time the words suited, the delivery accompanied by the push of his fingers behind the sharp fold of a collar, sliding along the warm skin underneath. Noah leveraged his weight against him, murmuring encouragement when Rett gasped at the contact, and slid one hand up the dark blue silk of the waistcoat. He feathered a fingertip over the inventive fastening at his ribcage. "This is beautiful," he said in quiet approval.

Rett's lashes fluttered, eyes still at half-mast as he watched Noah touch each button of the waistcoat and unhurriedly trace the placket of the shirt. His exhale was shaky when Noah calmly began to release the buttons at his throat. "I—" Rett swallowed thickly. "I dressed for dinner."

Noah laughed softly. "I see that." He smiled, hoping the racing beat of his heart was not distractingly loud, thankful he was only getting it at half volume. "I approve," he added, dipping to kiss the newly exposed hollow of throat. When he straightened, his eyes were serious. "I'm sorry I was late."

He felt the tremble in Rett's fingers when they brushed down the skin of his stomach to tug at his belt.

"You're forgiven," Rett finally said.

He pulled the belt from Noah's jeans, one long slide of leather through denim, discarding it to the floor.

"That's good." Noah's voice was unsteady in the best possible way. "That's really good."

And it was Rett's turn to laugh, before he pushed at Noah's stomach, backing him across the kitchen floor. "Do you want to eat now or later?"

Even if Noah had been starving, his answer would still be the same. "Later," he managed before Rett's mouth was on his and he was being guided through the dark pantry to the stairs.

That they made it to the bedroom at all was a miracle, but the sight of that giant bed gave Noah such a fit of butterflies that he laughed self-consciously when Rett pushed him down on the sheets.

"Why are you laughing?" Rett asked, mouth trailing over Noah's chest, lips turning up in a smile against the too-warm skin when he felt an immediate response.

Noah tugged at the buttons on the waistcoat. "Because you still make me nervous," he admitted, releasing the strange side fastenings and slipping the dark blue garment from Rett's shoulders. "I almost want to leave this on you." He let it fall gently to the floor.

"Gabriel will be pleased you enjoyed it."

Noah blinked, and then snorted, clapping a hand over his eyes, cheeks flaming. "Oh Jesus, you did *not* just imply a priest is…did…" He couldn't finish and bit his lip.

He jumped when Rett nudged at his mouth, relaxing into the offered kiss and winding his fingers into Rett's hair instead of hiding.

"I did more than imply," Rett said when he sat up, straddling Noah's hips and looking entirely too good while doing it. "Gabe has been playing cupid." He unbuttoned his cuffs, then the remaining buttons on his shirt, his fingers slow and methodical until Noah could take no more and brushed them away so he could do it himself.

A lot less steady but a lot more participatory.

"Gabe is a smart man," Noah muttered, nearly upending Rett when he sat up. He wound an arm around his waist to hold him in place and peeled the shirt from his shoulders. "I brought him pie."

He kissed the delicate curve of a collarbone.

"And I ruined it," Rett breathed, scratching his fingers down Noah's scalp, smiling at a rumble of pleasure.

"It probably still tastes amazing," Noah whispered against the softest of skin behind Rett's ear.

"I'm tempted to test your logic." Rett gasped as Noah experimentally sucked a thin margin of skin between his teeth.

"In a minute," Noah grunted, shifting Rett on his lap and rubbing his lips along the coarse stubble of Rett's jawline.

"This better take longer than a minute," Rett muttered irritably, swiveling his hips and making Noah's eyes cross, even as a light-hearted joy bubbled up in his throat.

Noah settled his hands on Rett's waist and grinned. "Well, I've got all night."

"That's good," Rett said, nodding seriously before shoving Noah to his back again. "That's very good."

Noah thought he was prepared for the feel of skin on skin, but when Rett lay down on top of him, aligning their bodies from shoulder to calf, he had to bite hard into his cheek to hold back a heartfelt groan. And when those beautiful dark wings draped over their heads, surrounding them in a fragrant tent of feathers, Noah closed his eyes and had to remind himself to breathe.

"Are you all right?" Rett teased, voice sultry and tinged with enough self-satisfaction that Noah felt compelled to retaliate.

He dragged all ten fingers down the center of Rett's back without warning.

Rett moaned, bucking into Noah's hands, wings trembling, chasing Noah's fingers as they combed through the feathers again. He collapsed onto Noah's chest, mouth dragging over his temple feverish and hot.

"I want you," he whispered against Noah's scars, lips caressing his ear, and Noah shuddered, feeling the words he could not hear.

"I don't have a clue what I'm doing," Noah admitted, hands skimming across Rett's bare shoulders to cup his face. He had been with men, but this was Rett, and he was different.

Rett shivered. "You're doing very well." He let Noah draw his mouth down and kissed him long and deep.

When he pulled back, he blinked so slow and sexy that Noah had to kiss him again. "What do you want?"

Rett studied him, gaze roaming over Noah's face and torso long enough that Noah wriggled self-consciously. "What do *you* want, Noah?" He lightly traced the curve of Noah's eyebrow until his fingertip met the pale line of healed skin.

Noah was blushing, he knew, his ears and neck burning with the excess heat, not all of it caused by the lips and hands of the man lying on top of him. But he threw caution to the wind and asked for what he wanted, for a change. "Lie down," he said gruffly, pushing lightly at Rett's hips.

Rett's eyebrows rose slightly but he slid off and settled onto his back, Noah following the movement, looming over him.

"God, you're gorgeous," Noah exhaled, and it was true. Rett's cheeks were flushed with color, his eyes so rich the blue was liquid, luminous. His wings spread out beneath them in a carpet of dense blue-black, and Noah knew he could (and dear *God* he hoped he would) spend an entire night buried in them and still not get enough.

But for now, he wanted to get his hands on the more human part of Rett, the part Rett might remember, the part he could more easily associate with what Noah's heart and body wanted him to learn, to know.

Even if Noah wasn't sure he was ready to say it aloud.

He lowered his head and pressed his lips to the center of Rett's chest. It wasn't his heart, but it was close, and Noah hoped the symbolism was clear. Rett's stomach trembled when Noah's mouth dragged over the muscles, tongue laving a path low and broad, swirling around hips and dipping into his navel.

Rett's hand had traveled to the nape of his neck while he explored, but it didn't urge or protest, it merely followed, the touch light and strangely soothing. Noah turned his head at one point and pressed his lips to the palm, meeting Rett's eyes before he began to pull his pants from his hips. He rubbed his head into Rett's open hand like a cat, and Rett obliged, cradling the crown of his head when he dipped his mouth to taste him for the first time.

There was a brief clench of fingers in his hair and a sharp intake of breath, and then Rett relaxed under Noah's mouth as he took him apart. He could feel Rett's frustration spike when he pulled away, leaving him brutally on the edge, and Noah smiled to himself when Rett finally, *finally*, lost all sense of his cool composure.

"*Noah*," Rett ground out between his teeth.

"I'm right here," Noah whispered, laughing when Rett pushed angrily at Noah's remaining clothes.

"Get these off," Rett growled, shoving Noah to his back and stripping the jeans efficiently from his legs. In an instant Noah was so overcome by sensation that he cried out, or at least he thought he did, his one good ear buzzing too loudly for him to be sure.

It was good, so good Noah was immobilized, all of his senses narrowing to a single point of pleasure directly correlated to the kiss-bruised lips that tugged ruthlessly, self-possessed. A white-hot stab of jealousy struck him unexpectedly, a quick-fire hatred leveled at some long distant and unknown lover, Rett's mouth too practiced, his movements too assured. The whole damned thing nearly came to an embarrassing halt until Noah recognized one quirky dip of Rett's head, a technique Noah knew was his own. His spike of fury diffused into a molten fondness that made every kiss more perfect.

Wanting more than he thought, more than he wanted to examine too closely, Noah tried to force his vocal cords to work when he really needed them, for once in his goddamned life. "Rett," he squeaked helplessly. "Rett, *baby,* wait." And the endearment was enough, Rett's exacting focus broken as he met his eyes.

"C'mere," Noah said low, tugging at Rett's bicep when he didn't immediately move. "Let me have this too."

Rett's intense frown softened into a smile and he crawled up Noah's body, plastering himself against him and crushing their mouths together.

Noah ran his hands lightly over the wing joints on his back, settling at his waist and while Rett kissed him senseless. "You're pretty good at that," he grinned, when Rett finally allowed him to suck in some much-needed oxygen. He traced the swollen skin of Rett's lower lip, slipping his thumb inside and catching his breath when Rett bit into the pad of the tip. "Is this your first time with a…" He couldn't finish, uncertainty clouding his voice.

His insecurity must have shown, because Rett's eyes were soft when he spoke. "Outside of an odd fantasy or two, yes."

Noah groaned at the implication of his words. "Have you thought about it, Rett? About me?" He couldn't resist pushing his thumb between Rett's lips again.

"Since the first night," Rett said carefully, after pulling Noah's hand from his mouth and kissing his palm.

"You can't just say things like that," Noah complained, voice husky. Although by Rett's answering smile he *could,* and Noah was exceedingly glad that he *did.* Especially if he did it while sucking the hell out of Noah's fingers, or any other part of his anatomy.

"Noah?" Rett rolled his hips restlessly against Noah's, biting his lip.

"Yeah, Rett," Noah said, brushing their mouths together. "I'm right here." Noah swallowed Rett's moan when he shuddered, hands gentle and guiding, until Rett began to arch away, overwhelmed. "Stay with me," Noah urged, holding him tight and giving him what his body craved, deft touch and soft whispers of encouragement obliterating any option that included panic or fear.

And when Rett finally tumbled over the edge, Noah was thankful for the fleeting moment that they had slowed, freeing doubts and uncertainties into the space between them, because the release was that much sweeter for it. He laughed a breathless warning when Rett grabbed the hand that still nestled them against his belly, but Rett didn't seem to mind and he linked their fingers with a shaky exhale and a kiss.

And they lay breathing together, boneless, night air sticky and humid and altogether wonderful in its damp closeness.

CHAPTER 13

*A*n obnoxious stomach gurgle broke the peaceful haziness between slumber and wakefulness and Noah laughed softly, trying to ease out from under the weight of Rett's arm. "Let me up."

"No," Rett mumbled, face mashed into Noah's shoulder. He dragged his mouth in place across the skin, touching his tongue to the salt-sweet taste that lingered there.

Noah huffed, kissing an apology into the nearest body part he could reach, the silky dark top of a mussed head. He pushed, gentle but insistent. "I promise I'll make it worth your while."

"Fine," Rett sighed dramatically, flopping to his back with some effort in a hypnotic rotation of luminous skin and dark feathers.

Noah swallowed, mouth suddenly dry. Even though he assumed he now had permission to look and touch at will, the entirety of *Rett* was a visual feast that he had trouble processing. Especially so close at hand and warmly inviting. "I'll be right back," he said gruffly, swinging out of bed before he did something stupid like wax poetic about the dark trail of hair that bisected Rett's taut stomach, or the glistening black layer of feathers between his body and the sheets.

He was still muttering under his breath as he padded across the floor when his neck prickled, alerting him that eyes tracked his departure. He glanced back to find Rett was plainly enjoying the view. "Stop that." He jabbed a finger in Rett's direction and slipped through the bathroom door, grinning at the deep chuckle that followed.

He wet a washcloth and took care of himself before snagging a towel and returning to bed. "You're kind of dirty for someone who *looks* like an angel," he offered, lips pursed as he climbed over Rett's naked hips.

"I'm no angel," Rett said dryly, eyes fluttering closed when Noah began to swipe him gently with the damp cloth. He tried to force Noah back onto the bed, yearning, but Noah slid off the mattress, ducking free of his grasp. "*Now* where are you going?" Rett asked peevishly.

Noah tossed the linens in a corner behind the door. "Don't move," he warned without answering. "I want you right there, just like that, when I get back."

Rett closed his eyes and tucked his wrists behind his head. "You have five minutes," he said, blithely unimpressed with Noah's rather anemic attempt at severity.

"Bossy, demanding," Noah muttered as he jogged down the steps. "Fucking *hot*."

The dark house was quiet, absent of the usual settling noises of evening. In the kitchen he found cold chicken and roasted potatoes in the refrigerator and added a generous portion of each to a chipped porcelain plate. The thin gold border of the china shone in the moonlight from the narrow kitchen window, a dignified contrast to the deep red of the rose pattern along the rim. He grabbed a fork from a drawer, the weight of the old silver heavy in his hand as he balanced his spoils on the top of the crushed pastry box. He paused when he reached the foot of the stairs in a surreal moment of contemplation.

He was standing naked in the foyer of a 200-year-old mansion, *in a swamp*, while an equally naked man *with wings*, waited for him in a giant bed upstairs.

He shook his head with a wide grin. *George would never believe this.* Then he immediately flushed because, *naked man with wings*, and began to climb.

"You were very nearly late." Rett was sitting up in bed, blessedly covered by a thin sheet.

"Funny," Noah said, setting the plate and box carefully at the end of the bed and leaning over to kiss him, thrilling that he could. *Finally.* "Are you hungry?" he asked, stealing another kiss, wondering how many he could manage before it became apparent he was addicted. He nudged Rett toward the center of the bed.

Rett frowned. There was an entire bed that Noah had but to walk around to reach, but he scooted over, making room. "I am famished," he answered, tone loaded and eyes hot as they skated over Noah's bare hip.

"Dirty," Noah retorted under his breath before he ducked under the sheet, slapping Rett's greedy hands away. "And I'm starved." He pulled the plate onto his lap first, tearing away a hunk of dark meat and popping it between his lips. "Mmmm," he hummed happily before offering a similar piece to Rett. "Compliments to the chef."

Rett sucked the meat from his fingers and Noah frowned when he whirled his tongue around the tips perhaps a second too long. "You're never going to play fair, are you?"

Rett shrugged and pressed slightly greasy lips to the back of Noah's hand. "No."

Noah snorted and pulled another piece of meat from the bone. "At least you're honest." He gave this bite to Rett too, deciding he liked the way he chewed, the motion of his jaw, the way his Adam's apple bobbled when he swallowed.

Jesus, he thought, a little faint. *I'm so screwed.*

They ate chicken and potatoes until the plate was clear, the still of the night broken by soft laughs and husky whispers and occasional deep grumbling when Noah insisted on feeding them both.

"I've got this," Noah murmured, gently shoving away yet another roving hand and lifting the lid on the cake box.

"I am not a child," Rett complained, before allowing Noah to soothe his temper with a long kiss.

"And thank God for that," Noah quipped, scooping a mash of crust, blueberries and lemon filling on the tines of the fork.

Rett laughed and Noah was entranced by the change in his face as he closed his lips around the pie. The lines around his eyes smoothed and softened, the tense planes of his jaw relaxed; he looked handsome and carefree and young.

"What are you staring at?" Rett asked self consciously, dabbing at his lips.

Noah flushed, realizing the fork was still poised between them. He shrugged, dipping into the box again. "You." He grinned when Rett's lips parted in anticipation, but took the bite for himself, moaning a low grunt of approval at the explosion of flavor on his tongue.

Rett frowned and grabbed the end of the fork, pulling it slowly from Noah's mouth.

Noah dragged his tongue along the length of it as it left his lips, winking at Rett's flustered expression.

"I believe I've waited long enough for my turn," Rett muttered, taking the box from Noah's lap.

"Hey!" Noah protested around flakes of pastry and fruit.

"You, Noah Hix." Rett used the fork to separate the pie into recognizable flavors. "Are a detriment to my peace of mind." He swirled the old silver in a marbled swath of lemon and flattened meringue, before holding it in front of Noah's lips in offering.

Noah opened his mouth and tipped forward.

Rett pulled the fork just out of reach. "You are also a glutton and clearly spoiled rotten."

Noah's mouth snapped shut, eyes darting from the fork to Rett's unyielding expression, patently unsure which was turning him on more. He decided he was content to play along rather than argue the fallacies in at least one of those statements and remained silent, parting his lips again when Rett brought the tines close.

Rett met him halfway, lips grazing his temple. "I would spoil you," he whispered and Noah strained to catch the words. "So much."

"Rett," he murmured, tilting his head back to meet the lips trailing over his cheekbone. He was rewarded with a savory mouthful of pie and a lengthy span of messy, tart kissing, lemon sucked from his tongue and his cheeks until his head spun. "I'm not spoiled," he said when he could finally breathe.

Rett's answering grin was soft and private.

"I'm *not*," he insisted. "You were probably a really good dad."

Rett froze, face blanking, and he was pulling away before Noah could stop him.

"Rett, no, wait." He clamped a hand around Rett's wrist in a vise, preventing him from fleeing entirely. They both paused, eyes falling on the forlorn box between them, until Rett finally relaxed, nodding once.

"I don't want to talk about that," he said in quiet apology, the hand holding the fork lowering to his lap.

Noah watched him try to cover his sorrow behind a cool façade, the effort spoiled by cheeks still flushed from exertion and easy laughter, and the hot summer night. And kissing. Noah pulled the forgotten fork from Rett's fingers. "Then we won't talk about it."

Rett looked up in surprise, troubled gaze clearing in gratitude and what appeared to be a glint of tenderness, different than the heat that so often preceded their usual interactions. Noah filed the shift away for later. He dipped into the pale yellow filling and held the fork in front of Rett's lips.

Rett accepted, swallowing before he spoke, words hesitant but gentle, a peace offering. "What would you like to talk about?"

Noah shrugged lightly, choosing a plump blueberry for himself. "What would you like to know?"

"Your brother, George," Rett said too quickly, and Noah thought maybe he wasn't the only one who had been harboring a growing interest.

"George." Noah smiled fondly, slipping a hefty chunk of meringue dipped crust through Rett's lips, unable to resist leaning over to suck a stray flake of sugar-coated pastry from the corner of his mouth. "He's my only brother, my only sibling. When he was little, he was this gangly, big eyed kid with too many teeth and too-long hair."

Rett smiled at the description, settling against the headboard for the reminiscence. He toyed with the sheet at Noah's hips, one eyebrow lifting as he teased it ever so slightly lower.

"Behave," Noah warned, pointing at him with the fork. He thought about George at six and fourteen and twenty-one and now, mourning how quickly the time had passed, how sharp the pain that still lingered sometimes, remembering his baby brother embracing the different stages of life. He wondered if that was what fatherhood felt like. "He's smart, was always smarter than me." He waited, but no interruption or polite but misguided protest ever came and for that he was thankful, appreciating Rett's simple willingness to listen.

"Our parents died in a car wreck when I was seventeen. George was thirteen. We lived with our dad's best friend after that, Dave." Noah's eyes were fogged with memories, his thoughts far away both in distance and years. "Then George went to college and I went to war," he ended on a sigh. The intervening years didn't matter much; they had shaped the people he and George had become, but there were things that couldn't be changed and ultimately no longer mattered.

"A soldier," Rett murmured, running a finger down the beaded chain hanging from Noah's neck, interrupting the melancholy train of his thoughts.

"Yeah," Noah nodded, blowing out the anxiety-riddled breath he'd been holding. "And George's a teacher now, an associate professor near Kansas City, where I live." His chest swelled with pride as he remembered George's college graduation. "He went to law school, passed the bar, and realized after about a year that he would rather be in the classroom." Noah laughed, shaking his head. "Better him than me."

"You would be an excellent teacher," Rett protested. "You are very patient, and kind. You exude a warmth and." He stopped and Noah would have sworn his cheeks visibly pinkened.

"And," Noah prodded teasingly, feeling his own skin tingle with the selfish pleasure of listening to Rett describe him.

"Happiness," Rett exhaled after a beat. "You, Noah, are light. As I am dark." He expanded a wing over their heads.

Noah glanced up before meeting Rett's somber gaze. "That must be why we work."

Rett blinked in surprise, then smiled softly and lowered the wing. He accepted a bite of pie when Noah offered it, chewing thoughtfully and watching the moonlight glint off a pair of brushed silver tags. "Tell me about your accident."

Noah lowered his head, studying the sad remains of the pie. He carefully closed the box and leaned over the side of the mattress to set it on the floor, fork resting diagonally on top. A hand slid over his bare hip and up his spine, followed by a pair of slightly sticky lips. He grinned when Rett tugged him down until he was flat on his back, and his breath hitched when a warm mouth sucked gently into the crease between his neck and shoulder, a hand pulling away the sheet that separated their skin. "Are we still talking?" he asked, biting his lip as the butterflies took off in his stomach again.

"Yes," Rett said the word against his neck, delicately dipping the tip of his tongue into the hollow of his throat. "Go on, I'll stop."

Noah caught him when he made as if to move away. "Don't you dare."

Rett smiled and pressed his mouth lightly to Noah's shoulder, a promise for later, but settling on the pillows beside him.

"It was..." Noah hesitated before scooting back against the headboard, feeling too exposed lying uncovered in the dark. No one had ever been so interested in what he had to say, about anything really, but most certainly not about the things that mattered. Rett was present in a noticeably tangible way. He listened without interrupting, absorbing all of Noah's words without judgment or opinion. It was heady and more than a little overwhelming. Noah tipped his chin toward the ceiling, his crown knocking against the polished mahogany, searching for the right narrative; for the first time since he had returned from the desert, he wanted to relive it long enough to share the burden of the memory.

"It was bleak. Scary." He laughed darkly. "I thought I was a hotshot. Tough kid, didn't care much for school. Lost both my parents in one split second and never even cried."

Rett rolled into his side and fit his palm at Noah's waist, sensing his need to be touched, grounded.

"But then I found myself in the middle of the desert, and it was hot and lonely and desolate." Noah smiled down at the face now nearly obscured in shadow. "There were spiders so big they *might* have given me a slight advantage when it came time to meet you."

Rett rubbed his chin thoughtfully against Noah's ribs, squeezing him when he shivered. "What do you mean?"

Noah laughed softly. "That tickles. And I'm talking measurable in feet, Rett. Not inches. The stuff of horror movies." He shuddered. "I hate spiders."

"As do I," Rett admitted solemnly and Noah snorted.

"So the first time I saw you, you weren't really that different, all things considered." Noah stroked the forearm that lay across his belly. "You were scary and unbelievable, and kind of beautiful." He trailed off, feeling a blush sneak across his skin. "And I'm a huge sap who should think before he speaks," he added ruefully.

"Thank you," Rett said quietly.

Noah squeezed his arm before continuing. "So, there I was, in the desert, bored out of my skull for the most part. Been there two and a half years, three fucking *weeks* from coming home," Noah blew out a hard breath. "And the transport chopper I was traveling in was shot down."

Rett sat up on an elbow and traced the scar on Noah's shoulder, pushing him gently forward so he could follow it down his back. "This too?"

"Uh huh," Noah nodded. Rett's fingers left needle points of electricity where they trailed the mottled edges of damaged tissue. "I was thrown to the ground before the whole damn thing exploded. Saved my life." He tapped his temple. "But it blew apart my inner ear, and the shrapnel tore me up pretty good. They said I was lucky I didn't lose the eye too."

His mind drifted into that faraway place of dark smoke and intense heat, of desert sand and falling, falling, falling; after a moment of quiet breathing Rett pulled him back into the present, urging him down to the bed again. When Noah was under him, Rett kissed the damaged eyebrow and shoulder and then his lips. "Then what?"

"I don't remember," Noah whispered, eyes closed, deciding that *feeling* was more important than thinking right now. "I dream about it, the smoke and the fire and the screams..." He stopped because that's all it was, all it *ever* was. "I was the only survivor," he admitted softly. "Me. Noah Hix, high school drop out."

Rett didn't know what the words meant, but he understood the sentiment behind them and he hushed him, soothing in the only way he knew how, with his hands and his mouth until Noah was distracted and tender, and they were both lost in what the other could give.

They fell asleep after, between long kisses and whispered laughter, the moon spilling over the bed in a pale mist of grey.

CHAPTER 14

*N*oah was startled awake by Gabriel's indignant squawk.

"Jesus, Mary and Joseph!" Gabe lamented, clapping a hand over his eyes.

When he didn't move from the bedroom doorway, Noah chuckled sleepily. "Sorry padre." He craned a hand around for the sheet but failed to locate it given his limited mobility. He shoved at the body draped over him. "Rett."

Rett grunted.

"Rett, move." Noah prodded his side.

Gabe stood rooted in place, muttering to himself, eyes still safely ensconced behind his palm. "But the broken glass," he said, voice small and confused.

"Foreplay," Rett grumbled, rolling off of Noah. He tossed the sheet behind him when Noah flailed wildly to cover up all the bits Rett's wings no longer hid.

"Oh God," Gabe said, backing blindly out of the room.

"I'm hungry!" Noah called. "If you're suffering from voyeur guilt!"

Rett opened one eye. "How can you possibly be hungry?"

Noah threw the free corner of the sheet over Rett's bare butt and snuggled up close. "I'm still recuperating," he said cheekily.

"It's too hot to cuddle." Rett's voice was muffled as he planted his face in the downy softness of the pillow.

"I'm not cuddling!" Noah protested, hooking one leg over Rett's thigh. He grinned when Rett's wing twitched as he ran a finger over the arch at the top. "You want to go cuddle in the shower?" He scratched a hard line down the center of Rett's back when he didn't immediately respond.

Rett growled, the deep sound vibrating through the mattress.

"Was that a yes?" Noah whispered, wondering if he could somehow dredge up the stamina to finish what he was about to start. On an empty stomach no less.

Rett raised his head to glare at him. "I'm tired. *Someone* didn't allow for much sleep last night."

Noah kissed his grumpy mouth. "You're really hot when you're mad." He wagged his eyebrows. "All that shower, Rett. You, me. Wet and naked."

Rett huffed and covered Noah's head in a flurry of feathers, pushing him down on the bed. "Go back to sleep."

"Hey," Noah chuckled. "Not fair." He breathed deep. God *damn* feathery Rett smelled good. He dug his fingers into the down and twisted lightly.

"Noah," Rett warned, yanking the wing back and sitting up in one fluid motion.

Noah blinked at his rapid change in position. "How do you do that?"

"I'm cursed. It has its perks."

Noah's laughter rang out, echoing down the stairs and into the kitchen.

Gabe grinned, kneeling over the dustpan and sweeping up the last of the glittering shards. He shook his head. "Today is shaping up to be a beautiful day."

"I DON'T UNDERSTAND the point of this lesson," Rett said stiffly, poking the black rectangle apprehensively.

Noah rolled his eyes. "Pick it up and I'll show you." He pecked out a text message with his thumbs and the phone in front of Rett lit up, jiggling across the table as it buzzed excitedly.

Rett peered at the lit screen but didn't touch the phone.

"Rett." Noah said in exasperation.

Noah: *This is a text message. It's 21st century letter writing.*

Rett studied the message thoughtfully and then glanced at Noah. "And how do I respond?"

Noah hid his grin. *I've got you now,* he thought. He might have been secretly plotting about a hundred dirty text messages in the aftermath of last night. "Well, first you have to *touch it.*" He looked pointedly at the phone on the table.

Rett sighed and gingerly picked up the device in one hand, his face clearly expressing distrust. When it didn't do anything remarkable after several seconds, he raised his eyes to Noah's. "Make it write again."

"No. You have to answer me first. That's how it works. I text you," Noah nodded to the phone. "And then you text me back."

Rett frowned in consternation. "I don't know how."

"Look," Noah leaned over the table and pointed at the keys. "Each letter is here. You just press them to type. Like this." He was upside down, but he started a simple reply. "And then you hit this arrow to send it to me."

"Hmm," Rett sniffed and slapped Noah's hand away. "I can do that."

Noah chuckled. "I figured." He sat back in his chair and waited. While Rett carefully picked out letters on the tiny keyboard, his eyes fell on the dishes soaking in the sink and the sun shining the bright yellow of Indian summer in the back yard. Gabriel had cleaned up the broken glass before cooking breakfast, although he had gone back to his little house before they had emerged from the shower.

Noah suppressed a shiver recalling the hour *after* he had coaxed Rett from bed.

That shower was definitely built for two.

And Rett, naked, wet, dark wings dripping as they pinned Noah against the tile wall, was a sensory overload Noah was pretty damn excited to repeat just as soon as his sore and tired body had recovered.

He was going to be the cleanest goddamn mechanic this side of the Mississippi.

The phone in his hand buzzed.

Rett: *Thank you for the phone and the brief lesson in 21st century letter writing. I appreciate your restraint in the amount of sarcasm used during instruction. I would like to take this opportunity to retract my earlier statement about you being a wonderful teacher.*

Noah snorted. "You're hilarious."

Rett raised his eyebrows, waiting.

"Okay, okay," Noah muttered, typing quickly.

Noah: *Shut up. I'm an excellent teacher. You would have never even thought to use that coconut lotion in your shower that way before I showed you.*

Rett's lips pursed.

Rett: *Erroneous.*

Noah grinned. *Juicy. Do tell, flyboy.*

Rett: *Tell or show? Or perhaps you would prefer both; a narrated tale.*

Noah: *I'm going to be sorry I got you this phone, huh?*

Rett: *Probably.*

Noah snorted and flapped his fingers. "Ok, give it to me. That's enough." He shifted in his seat, jeans a little tighter than when he sat down twenty minutes ago.

"No, it's mine," Rett said with a frown, holding it out of reach. He waved to the back door. "You should go work on your car now. I'll take care of the dishes."

"You know damn good and well you just want to ogle my ass as I walk out," Noah said drily but he stood anyway, tight crotch be damned. He leaned over the table and Rett obliged, stretching to give him a long kiss. "I'll be outside," Noah said a little breathlessly. "Working on my car."

Rett nodded solemnly. "I'll be inside. Ogling your ass through the upstairs window."

Noah laughed and wiped his hand across his mouth self-consciously. "You really are a monster." He swallowed the impulse to drag Rett down on the partially cleared kitchen table and have a go at round four. "I'll just be outside then." He ignored Rett's smugly satisfied look as he stepped through the screen.

His phone buzzed before he was halfway to the Road Runner.

Rett: *It is very hot. You should remove your shirt.*

Noah laughed. It was going to be a good day.

It took Rett less than two days to master the cell phone, including the camera function.

Noah made very little progress on the car.

Gabriel baked an assortment of pies.

On the third night, Noah had his first nightmare in several days, but this time when he awoke with a scream on his lips and the panicked closure in his throat, someone was waiting, wrapping around him, easing breath back into his lungs with a kiss. The dream faded much quicker than before, Noah discovered, chased away by the warm closeness of another body and whispered assurances across his skin. It was a release in a way it never had been, and as sleep reclaimed him Noah wondered if he would ever have the dream again.

He was changing the socket on his wrench, leaning against the driver's side door when his new phone jangled from the top tray of the toolbox.

George: *How goes the repairs grease monkey?*

Noah smiled. "Smartass," he muttered. *They go, professor. How's everything at home without me there to hold it together?*

He frowned when George didn't immediately reply and held the phone in the shade provided by the side of the car, wondering if he had lost service. He was lucky to get two bars over most of the property. When it buzzed again, he sighed in relief, only to find it wasn't from George.

Rett: *I would like to have lunch now.*

Noah grinned and tapped out a reply. *Yes, your highness.*

Rett: *All subjects must do the bidding of the royal in residence. You do realize.*

Noah: *Well I was hoping.*

Rett appeared in the yard in that eerie, invisibly silent way of his and Noah's heart may never get over the initial shocked thump before Rett was pushing him into the shade under the eaves and crushing their mouths together. Noah moaned a little, hot and sweaty and hands full of smooth skin and a fine layer of feathers and *Christ*, but he was getting desperate for this, the minutes and hours that passed between the last time they were together and now, each increment getting shorter but somehow more distracting and need-filled.

A car horn startled them both and Noah jumped back, eyes going immediately to the bayou and beyond, where the gravel road waited, still inaccessible.

A tall figure stood beside a familiar wrecker, one arm raised in a broad wave.

"George," Noah breathed, face slack in a mixture of shock and joy.

Rett sank deep into the darkness provided by the corner overhang of the roof, reconciling his need to touch Noah with the need to hide.

"Wait," Noah reached for him, hands falling through the humid air as Rett escaped along the chipping exterior paint. "Rett, wait."

"Your brother," Rett finally said, pausing only because the voice that urged him to stop had become too vital, his familiar opposition having vanished, lost somewhere between the kitchen or the yard or their bed.

"Just," Noah bit his lip, trying to process the rapid turn of events, swallowing a sinking feeling in the pit of his stomach that said somehow he and Rett had turned a corner too sharp, misguided, and now they weren't going to make the curve. "Let me go talk to him, okay? Jesus," he exhaled, mind reeling. "How the fuck did he find me?"

"Go, I'll be in the house." Rett was a calm voice of reassurance, and then he was gone, slipping around to the rear entrance, wings shadowed, green glint obscured without the buttery touch of sun.

"Yeah, okay," Noah said to the faded white wall before he started across the yard, each step stinging with a hint of failure, though at what he couldn't be quite sure. "Georgie!" he called excitedly when he was close enough, brushing aside the disquiet and concentrating on his gladness. His eyes widened when a second, smaller figure joined his brother at the door of the truck.

"How the hell you managed to end up trapped in the back forty of nowhere is beyond me." George raised his voice over the rush of the water, wide grin on his face. He patted Max on the head and she swatted him away. "We were beginning to think the locals were playing a joke on the tourists when they drew us that map!"

Noah didn't miss the barely concealed relief in his brother's eyes. "Long story, you wouldn't believe me if I told you."

"Who was the guy?" Max asked and there was something in her tone that put Noah on alert.

"He owns the house," he said evenly, feeling the strain of carefully kept composure, ignoring the probable futility of the effort.

Max's expression showed that she was well aware Noah was sharing only a portion of the truth, and the specifics were probably ten times more volatile than he was revealing. "Uh huh."

George elbowed her in the side. "Come on, Max," he laughed. "Don't mind her, she's still cranky because she got car sick about twenty miles back."

"I did not," Max huffed, shoving back.

Noah frowned. "You never get car sick."

"Oh my *God*," she groaned. "Would you two lay off? For pity sake, I'm *fine*."

"Calm down," Noah soothed. "You're awesome. And apparently still a master tracker. How the hell did you two find me?"

George grinned and reached through the open window to retrieve a familiar pink cake box. "Benny's? You bragged about the pie. I figured you were on a first name basis with all the short order cooks in town by now."

Noah laughed and shook his head, but a flash of guilt unsettled him; Rett's anger and concern had been warranted. If Benny had no qualms revealing his location to George, how long before he told others? What gossip had already swelled because of Noah's presence?

Eventually the idea would germinate that the old Rosewood house was no longer off limits for exploration. What would happen to Rett, and Gabe, when he was gone?

"Okay, so we're here. Now how do we get across?" Max interrupted the worrisome track of Noah's thoughts. "Fly?"

Noah's eyes met hers and he felt the hair rise on the back of his neck; she knew. He didn't know how she could possibly have seen anything from her vantage in the wrecker, but he had also learned long ago not to underestimate Maxine VanAsche. "Hang tight and I'll go figure out the best way to get you over to my side of paradise." He winked and hoped his false optimism would hold water.

"And bring me a beer! I'm thirsty!" George called, as Noah waded through the thick grass of the gently sloped incline.

When he looked back before he rounded the corner for the kitchen door, George and Max were sitting on the bed of the wrecker, sharing whatever Benny had provided in the box. "If that's pie, they by God better save me some," he grumbled.

Rett wasn't in the kitchen, or the pantry or foyer, the house too quiet, its dark stillness a symbol of its age and the absence of life and home. Noah slowed as he climbed the quiet stairs, a heaviness clenching at his heart; George and Max's appearance meant his time here was coming to an end. It was strange how the thought was not as welcoming as it might have been a few short days ago.

He found Rett in the bedroom, familiar and beautiful, framed by the windowpanes in the midday light as he watched over these new visitors to the bayou, the same as he had probably done countless times before.

"I will carry you across the water, down the bend and through the woods where we won't be seen."

Noah shook off the brief start of alarm at the unexpected words, smiling sadly at the easiness of Rett's delivery. "No," he said, quiet and firm.

Rett turned, mouth drawn tight in a frown, eyes shadowed. "What else would you have me do? Allow you to wade into that godforsaken swamp in another misguided and foolish show of bravery?"

Noah walked slowly to the window, ignoring the magnetic pull of the other man as he passed. His eyes followed the snaking shape of the river, still dangerously high, moss dripping from the trees in a curtain of grey against the lushness of the greens and browns. He studied the view, Rett's penance, wondering if it had changed at all in the century just passed, or the one preceding. He turned his back on it, hands comfortingly steady as they reached for the handsome face beside him, soothing the confusion and anguish he could feel thrumming beneath the skin. When he kissed him, Rett sighed into his mouth, a whisper soft exchange of breath that Noah took, gladly.

"What are you doing?" Rett murmured, lower lip clinging to Noah's when he pulled away as though the skin itself was coaxing a reversal of their parting.

Noah chewed the inside of his cheek, nervous. "I thought you might carry George and Maxie over here, to our side," he finally said, holding his breath, thumbprint dragging against the darkened jaw.

Rett closed his eyes and they were suspended in that moment, tethered together by the touch of Noah's hand. "What you ask," Rett pulled free of Noah's grasp, feeling the loss all the way to the bone, as the fingers fell from his face. "What you ask may hurt us both."

Noah watched Rett war with the request, emotions playing across his features and shadowing his eyes. Noah reached for him again, not in persuasion, but because he needed to be touching him when they did this, refused to give that up, unwilling to acknowledge the significance. Not yet. He tugged at slim hips until they nestled against his own, until they were wrapped in each other, arms and wings and mouths, a tangle of heat and breath, and Rett relented, laughing silently into Noah's neck.

"You are a scoundrel, Noah Hix, and a worthy opponent," he mumbled.

"I'm sorry," Noah said softly, and he had never felt the meaning behind the sentiment more strongly. No matter how George reacted, or Max, there was no easy ending to their story and the countdown had begun.

Noah didn't belong here.

Rett straightened and when his gaze met Noah's, his eyes were clear, the blue fierce and shining. "I'm not."

Noah's throat tightened. *Neither am I,* he thought, but he couldn't force the words past his lips. He sucked oxygen in shallow sips, pulse too fast, as Rett led him from the room and down the steps, hands warm and solid and entwined. When they reached the front door, Noah hesitated. "Give me about ten minutes? Fifteen at the outside? Might be better if I try to explain, what to expect."

Rett's smile was thoughtful. "I suppose I don't have time to arrange a heroic rescue from Earl."

"Don't even joke about that," Noah shuddered. He was consumed with a desire to kiss him again, to push Rett against the door and remember how good it was between them, reassure them both that nothing had changed. He paused, hand on the knob, until he had waited too long, until he was no longer sure Rett would welcome the reminder. He cleared his throat self-consciously. "Fifteen minutes. Then come down and I'll introduce you to my little brother."

Rett's solemn expression softened at Noah's choice of wording and he nodded.

CHAPTER 15

"Jesus Christ," George exhaled, eyes as wide as saucers. His mouth worked as he looked at Noah and then at Max and then back at the winged man standing beside his brother across the river. "Jesus fucking *Christ*."

Max snorted. "You said that already."

Noah didn't need even his rudimentary lip reading skills to comprehend the exchange. "You done?"

"I'm. I, uh." George stuttered and raked his hands through his hair, tugging at the roots until it hurt, as if to assure himself he was awake. "I'm speechless."

Noah rolled his eyes. "Don't mind George's theatrics, Rett, what he's trying to say is *Hello, it's very nice to meet you.*" He glared at George pointedly.

Max snickered, so Noah glared at her too.

George blinked. "Can I touch him?"

Noah choked. "Oh my God, George, no!"

"Yes," Rett said matter-of-factly before shooting over the bayou and landing lightly on his feet, an arms breadth away from the hood of the truck.

"Holy shit," Max whispered. Her cheeks were reddened from the hot midday sun and loose blonde strands stuck to her forehead where they had escaped her ponytail.

"Hey!" Noah called, perturbed at the glint he thought he could read in George's eyes as he approached a very still and serious Rett. "God damn it," he muttered. He knew Rett was playing along, trying to assuage George's concerns, but more than that he was doing what he thought Noah wanted him to do.

Not that Noah harbored any real fear about George, or Max.

He ground his teeth together when George ran a hand over Rett's left wing and it fluttered in response, feathers ruffling and shifting under his touch. George circled Rett, bolder, lightly touching the fine down at his neck.

Noah shifted his weight impatiently. When George reached for the joint over the scapular region, he had had enough. "For fuck's sake George, it's not a goddamn petting zoo!"

George dropped his hand guiltily. "Sorry," he said meekly and returned to Max's side.

"Noah has become accustomed to these." Rett raised the dark appendages. "He forgets that he once was just as fascinated as you."

"Accustomed, huh," Max hummed, rocking back on her heels. She glanced over the bayou to where Noah was pacing a worn path through the grass.

"So how do we do this?" George asked nervously.

Max rolled her eyes at his barely contained excitement. She waved with a dramatic flourish. "Ladies first," she smirked, indicating George should take the honor.

"Very funny," George said dryly, but he couldn't hold back a grin when Rett held out a hand.

A few seconds later he was staring up at the bluest sky he had ever seen. It would have been perfect except for Noah's giant head blocking the yellow warmth of the sun.

"The landing's a bitch, ain't it?" Noah grinned.

"Shut up," George groaned, brain scrambled as he tried to decide if Rett unceremoniously dumping him on the riverbank was payback for the groping or some bayou rite of passage. He scowled when Rett deposited Max gently beside Noah, steadying her on her feet before he released her. "Why didn't Max get thrown to the ground like last week's garbage," George grumbled. He shoved Noah's proffered hand away irritably.

"She's—" Rett stopped at Max's sharp look. "A lady," he finished with a little bow.

Noah's mouth watered at the combination of pretty manners and the return of the white shirt; Rett had put it on while he waited for Noah to explain things to his brother, probably in an attempt to appear presentable. The crisp collar did things to Noah's midsection, and his fingers twitched with a flash of sense memory, the smooth feel of the linen under his hands tangible and inviting.

"Noah!" Max snapped her fingers in front of his face.

Noah blinked. "What?"

"Uh, stranger? No wings, two o'clock?" Max pointed over his shoulder.

Noah glanced back and grinned, slapping his forehead. "Oh God, sorry. Gabriel."

Gabe expression was filled with uncertainty as he approached the group, perplexed by Rett's unusual show of hospitality to the strangers in their yard.

Noah Hix, it seemed, changed everything.

"George, Maxie, this is Gabriel, former priest and current master gardener. And carpenter," Noah winked.

Gabe didn't miss the nervous flutter of Noah's movements and he tried to decipher the significance of this exchange. He only wished his own future didn't hinge so purely on the heart of the former soldier standing in front of him. He had grown fond of Noah, exceptionally so, and it would be hard to see him leave under any circumstances. Knowing that Noah's exit had just been hastened by the appearance of these strangers, likely circumventing the end of two hundred years of tragedy and loss, made his words more cool than they might otherwise have been.

"How do you do," he said, taking first the girl's small hand, enjoying a flash of humor at her firm grip, before turning to the man.

His eyes widened as they traveled up, and up, before they met sparkling hazel eyes and cheeks flushed with excitement. Or maybe the heat; he couldn't be sure.

Gabriel swallowed.

George quirked an eyebrow, glancing at Noah in confusion.

Noah poked Gabe on the shoulder. "Padre."

"Sorry," Gabe started, thrusting his hand forward and accepting George's handshake. "Father Gabriel." He cringed. *Why did he introduce himself as a priest?*

Rett snorted, then hid his smile at Gabe's frown.

"George Hix," George grinned and shook the strange little man's hand enthusiastically. "You're a priest?"

"Holy as they come," Noah teased jovially, slapping Gabe on the back before gesturing for the group to head up the hill to the house. Rett fell naturally in step beside him until Max nudged her way between them, peppering Rett with questions.

"So, Rett. Are you married?"

"Max," Noah groaned.

"It's all right, Noah."

The rest of Rett's reply was lost in a gust of humid wind. George fidgeted when Gabriel didn't seem inclined to follow the group. "Maybe we should?" George asked, tilting his head in the direction of the house.

Gabe blinked and glanced around. "Oh! Sorry," he muttered, turning too quick and tangling his right foot in a knot of dense under-growth. He pitched forward and George caught him by the biceps just before Gabe face planted in his chest.

"Careful now," George said. He grinned when Gabe's cheeks flushed bright pink. "You okay?"

Gabe took two giant steps back, the imprint of George's fingers on his skin oddly tingling and warm. "I'm fine. Thank you," he said stiffly, inclining his head and striding purposefully through the grasses.

When he tripped over a rock forty yards later, George kept him on his feet again, one hand to his elbow.

Gabe sent a prayer heavenward that he be allowed to die immediately.

No one answered.

~

"But I don't understand how the curse will be lifted," George said, chewing thoughtfully.

Three occupants of the dining room froze.

"Buzzkill," Max whispered.

George glanced around guiltily. "Sorry," he winced. "Did I overstep?"

"I'm—I'm not really clear on that myself," Noah said. He watched Rett school his expression.

Rett set his fork on his plate with a sigh. "I'm not entirely sure, either." He looked at Gabriel. "Are you?" he asked, frustration coloring his tone. "Now? After this," he waved his hand to encompass the room, but Gabe knew he was encompassing one person in particular.

Gabe shook his head. "No. But obviously we're missing something important."

If Rett flinched, Noah pretended not to see it, the knot that had been forming in the center of his chest all afternoon a confusing sensation of fear and hope and failure. "Well, maybe if you tell us everything, we can figure it out. Together."

"No." Rett's response was quick.

Noah bristled. "What do you mean, *no*? If I can help, if *we* can help, Rett, then why not let us? I mean, what could it hurt?"

Rett's eyes were snapping and dark in the candlelight and Noah wanted to look away from their intensity but he forced himself to take it, neck heating as he remembered that same focus directed at him, on him. *God, he's gorgeous when he's angry,* he thought, wishing stupidly they were alone so he could goad Rett into a fight and then make it up to him after.

"Nevermind my own rather obvious imperfection, would you have me risk Gabriel's *life?*" Rett finally asked, throwing his cream linen napkin on the table, knocking over an empty water glass.

"Okay, okay," George soothed, hands waving Rett back into his seat. "You two been at it like this all week?"

"Yes," Gabe offered with a dejected sigh and George laughed.

"Padre, we can swap Noah stories later," he winked.

Gabe's mouth snapped shut and he looked quickly away from the handsome fellow seated unfortunately to his left. Unfortunate because his damnably muscular forearm brushed Gabe's every time he reached for his water, and Gabe was never sure if he was supposed to grit his teeth and bear it, or if he would be forgiven for scooting his chair a few inches closer.

He had barely eaten a bite.

"You've hardly touched your food," George said. He reached for his water glass and smiled kindly when Gabe snatched his arm from the table.

"I'm not hungry," Gabe lied. He was starving, but his stomach was jumping nervously and he really wanted nothing more than to go back to his little house and hide under his scratchy wool blankets until morning.

Max watched the entire tableau with a long-suffering scowl. Noah and Rett were still glaring at each other, and if the too-high color along the top of Noah's cheekbones was any indication, he was about three point five seconds from letting his beastly boyfriend take him upstairs and show him who was really the boss. Meanwhile, to her left, Professor Hix's shampoo model good looks had provided about a month's worth of confessional material for a two hundred year old Catholic priest.

She was going to bed.

"I'm going to bed," she said, disgruntled, shoving back from the table. "Bedroom?" She asked when the men around the table stared at her with uncertainty, save Rett who shot to his feet and gave a tiny bow.

"You may use Noah's bedroom," Rett said, tone formal.

Jesus, Noah thought, *he's sexy as hell.*

"I'm not even going to ask," Max muttered and left the room ahead of Rett when he gestured.

George studied Noah's nervous movements thoughtfully. "Are we bunking somewhere else then?"

"I will bring clean linens," Gabe offered stiffly and stood. He blinked when George rose too.

"Thanks, Gabe."

Gabe ignored the friendly grin and made it all the way into the yard before he stumbled and fell.

He lay on his back in the grass looking up at a twinkling sky full of stars, a stranger's kind eyes and pretty smile heating his middle in an altogether wonderful and frighteningly new way. "Fucking hell," Gabe muttered under his breath.

IT WAS LONG past midnight when George's soft snores finally alerted Noah that his brother was asleep.

Noah eased out of the bed they were sharing and padded silently from the room. He paused outside of Rett's cracked door, smiling at the sliver of moonlight that spilled into the hall, knowing it was as bold an invitation as he was likely going to get.

"Why are you still dressed?"

Noah jumped when lips touched the back of his neck. "Damn it, Rett," he whispered, shuddering when hands made quick work of the button and zipper of his fly. He shivered at the first touch of fingers on his skin.

"What took you so long?" Rett kissed the words between his shoulder blades, sucking small bites of skin between his teeth, hands pulling Noah free from his undergarments.

"George," Noah gasped, head lolling back, grasping at Rett's bare thighs for purchase, needing an anchor as sensation overwhelmed his body. *"Fuck."*

"Take these off," Rett ordered, flicking one of his hands at the waistband hanging loose around Noah's hips, the other hand reacquainting with velvety soft skin and hard smoothness and repeating all the touches that made Noah's breath catch in his throat.

"Can't," Noah shook his head, unwilling to move. "And don't you even think of stopping," he added between embarrassingly rapid draws of humid night air.

Rett chuckled darkly against his neck and traced his tongue along the juncture of his throat, priming the area for a gentle kiss before biting into it and sucking hard.

Noah groaned loudly, knees buckling and Rett caught him fast around the waist.

"Stay with me," Rett whispered against his ear, but Noah shook his head again.

"Can't hear you," he mumbled, eyes closed against the onslaught. His lungs burned, on fire, before he remembered to breathe.

Rett petted and soothed him, coaxing him back to lucidity with soft touches and warm lips, holding their bodies snugly together as he guided them to the bed.

Noah had the sense to lose the rest of his clothes before he fell into the sheets. "Give me five minutes," he said with a sultry grin.

Rett laughed softly and lowered himself on top of him, their bodies slotting together, chiseled pieces of the same whole. "I'll just wait here, then," he said cheekily, sucking lazily at Noah's neck.

Noah sighed, contented and relaxed, arms heavy when he lifted them to wrap around Rett so that he could rake his fingers over the sensitive bits of his wings.

Rett smiled down at him, teeth flashing in the moonlight as he ran his hands over Noah's flat stomach. "I like this."

Noah squirmed at the slow-moving fingertips, fisting one hand in the sheets. "You would," he muttered, secretly enjoying being outmaneuvered. Rett was ticking off all of his hidden kinks as sure as if he were going down a list.

"Where is this *'stuff'* you've mentioned you keep in your wallet?" Rett asked with a bawdy wink. "And more importantly, are you going to elaborate?"

Noah's mouth was dry as Rett slid off of the bed. In the few days they had been together, Rett had granted him carte blanche to touch and taste at will. But that body, over him, in him, that was the big one. And Noah was finally going to have it.

"I'm unfortunately not really an expert," Noah quipped when he found his tongue.

Rett triumphantly lifted Noah's wallet from his jean's pocket and tossed it on the bedclothes. He crawled over to where Noah sat and kissed him. "We'll figure it out," he said with such confidence that Noah laughed.

"I love you," he said with wide grin.

Rett froze.

Noah's lips parted, his mind a dizzying kaleidoscope of color and sound and a week's worth of tiny moments. He didn't know where the words had come from; they were just there, waiting to be spoken. And, even more surprising, he meant them. His hands tightened on Rett's waist.

"I love you," he said again, closing the distance between their mouths.

Rett let Noah kiss him, overcome. He couldn't breathe. By the time he had processed the weight of the moment, Noah was pulling away.

"What are you not telling me, Rett?" Noah whispered. "What happens after two hundred years?"

But Rett cut him off, capturing his lips in a hungry, desperate attempt to claim the man beneath him, body and soul, heart breaking because he had found at last the key to unlocking his every secret desire in the form of a soldier as lonely as he.

The wings remained, hovering above them in the large bed, telling him that somehow, it wasn't enough.

CHAPTER 16

*M*ax rushed into the bedroom, face pale, hair clinging to her cheeks in damp strands. "Bathroom," she barked at the jumble of blankets and feathers on the bed.

Noah lifted his head, blinking sleepily, and pointed.

Rett winced when the bathroom door slammed with enough force to rattle the window glass. "In a house this size you would think a man might enjoy a little privacy," he mumbled into Noah's neck.

Noah chuckled, petting the forearm wrapped snugly around his chest. "You get used to it." He squirmed when he felt the change in Rett's breathing pattern just before a lingering kiss was placed behind his ear. "Rett," he warned under his breath.

Rett sighed and released him, allowing space between them. "She's sick."

"What?" Noah's head quirked as he listened for any telltale signs. "How do you know?"

"I can hear her." He ran a fingertip over Noah's scarred temple.

Noah frowned and rolled out of bed.

"Noah—"

"I'll be right back," Noah reassured him, knocking once perfunctorily on the door before walking in.

143

"Go away," Max moaned, cradling the bowl of the toilet.

Noah pulled a washcloth from the shelf by the door and ran it under a cold stream of water in the sink, filling a glass before crouching beside her on the tile.

"You're an asshole," Max muttered, words echoing hollowly against the porcelain.

"So you keep telling me," Noah soothed, folding the cool, wet cloth and gently laying it across the back of her neck. He nudged the glass of water into her hand. "Rinse."

"Uh uh," Max shook her head miserably, but Noah noted the way she sank into the warmth of his knee at her back. Her shoulders were trembling.

"Rinse like a good girl and I'll let you drive the car home."

Max lifted her head, eyes bleary and red-rimmed. "Liar." But she took the water and swished and spit twice before pushing it away again.

She sagged against him and he caught the folded terrycloth square before it slid to the floor. He sighed and sat back against the wall, pulling Max into his lap, wiping her clammy brow with the damp washcloth. "So. Who do I cock my shotgun at? And please don't tell me it's the shaggy haired dude down the hall. I don't think there's enough bleach in the world to rinse that image from my brain."

"Shut up," Max snickered pitifully, burying her nose in Noah's neck. He smelled good, like warm, salty caramels and hot chocolate. "Why are all the good ones taken, Noah?"

Noah frowned when he felt something wet roll down his throat and onto his chest.

"Everything all right?" Rett asked quietly from the doorway.

To Max's credit, she didn't even flinch and Noah gave her a soft squeeze. That was his girl; she had walked in on her surrogate big brother in bed with a (winged) man, and hadn't so much as batted an eye. "Yup, we'll be right out."

"Max, do you feel you could eat something?"

"No," she groaned, as though the mere words were her death knell.

"I'll be back," Rett said to Noah before slipping out of the bathroom.

"He's too pretty for you," Max muttered thickly against his chest, the words accompanied by a loud sniff.

Noah snorted. "He's too something, all right," he agreed. He jiggled her easily into a more comfortable position; she was such a scrappy thing, tiny knuckles dangerous and sharp, feet too quick and aim too precise, he forgot how small she was in reality. "And don't change the subject. Spill the beans, Maxine."

Max sighed deeply but refused to look at him, and when she spoke, Noah understood why. "Tyler," was her muffled, nearly unintelligible reply.

But not unintelligible enough.

"Tyler *Littlejohn?*" Noah nearly tossed her to the floor, but caught himself when she whimpered.

Max nodded dejectedly and if her face hadn't been tinged a sickly pea green when she finally raised her sad eyes to meet his, Noah might have held onto his disgust a little bit longer.

He gritted his teeth and breathed through his nose to calm himself. "Tyler is a raging douchebag asshole, Max," he ground out.

"If you would have given him half a chance," Max began.

"You mean before or after he threw me in the clink?" Noah's voice bounced off the cold tile walls.

"You broke his nose."

"Yeah, well he had his hands all over you," he scowled, remembering the crunch of fist on bone with a tiny spurt of satisfaction.

"We were on a date!" Max shouted, then winced and grabbed her stomach. "I'm going to be sick," she whispered.

Noah held her hair while she dry heaved over the toilet. He patted her back soothingly, grumbling under his breath. "Does George know?"

"God, no!" Max said, voice husky as she collapsed into Noah's lap again. "For a smart dude, he's shockingly obtuse."

Noah chuckled. "Well then I can stop playing the overprotective big brother. Because George is going to *kill* him."

"I know," Max said glumly.

They sat on the cold floor of the bathroom, the quiet *drip drip* of the faucet the only sound.

"Is he divorced yet?" Noah finally asked, the million-dollar question and his biggest beef with the relationship from the start. Tyler Littlejohn, handsome, well-spoken, with hot dark eyes only for Max, had appeared in their midst last winter when he had been assigned a cold case. In a roundabout way, the Red Barn, Max's mother's establishment, had been a key factor in the case and Tyler had become a regular fixture in the bar, both on duty and off.

After he had solved the case and received a commendation from the chief of police, he hadn't disappeared, much to George and Noah's chagrin. No, he continued to shamelessly flirt with what amounted to their baby sister, even though he apparently still had a wife somewhere back east. Separated or not, to Noah's mind, married was married.

Then Noah broke his nose. He and Tyler had never really come back from that.

"I told him not to bother contacting me until he had the paper in his hand," Max whispered.

"And how long ago was that?"

Max's face crumpled. "Four weeks."

"So he has no idea."

Max shook her head wordlessly.

"Max—"

"I brought you some ginger tea," Rett interrupted quietly. "Do you think you might be up to a sip or two? It will calm your stomach."

"No," Max mumbled stubbornly into Noah's chest.

"Yes," Noah countered, reaching for the steaming mug Rett offered. "We're having a baby," he added, as he held the mug to Max's chapped lips.

"Yes, I know." Rett quirked one eyebrow when Noah shot him a look of surprise. "You didn't?"

Noah huffed lightly. "You did?"

"I thought it rather obvious."

Noah met his eyes over the top of Max's blonde head, felt the physical weight of the wistfulness in Rett's words. Wondered what it would take to convince the other man to allow him to share his long held burdens; knew it was probably foolish to want to. "Want to help me get her into bed?"

Rett nodded and took the mug, helping the two to their feet and following when Noah guided Max into the bedroom. Noah urged her onto the oversized mattress and pulled the blankets up to her neck before climbing in after her. When Rett stared down at them, perplexed, Noah reached out a hand, tugging hard when Rett took it, tumbling him onto the bed with them.

"I'm staying right here for the rest of the year," Max murmured, burrowing deep under the covers.

Noah wrapped an arm around her, blankets and all, and grinned sardonically. "You don't think *Detective Littlejohn* might have an issue with that?" He yawned contentedly when Rett finally seemed to understand that this was a thing that was happening and relaxed behind him, settling a great, dark wing over the trio in a protective curtain. "We already know his bloodhound skills are medal-worthy."

"You have about two hours to get that out of your system before I feel more like myself," Max warned faintly, voice waning as she fought sleep.

"I'm not worried," Noah lied, kissing her temple and listening to her shallow breaths, quiet and even. *Tyler,* he scowled. Motherfucker better do right by his girl or Noah was going to break more than his nose this time.

"There is a part of this story I am missing," Rett said softly, lips warm against Noah's cheek.

"Mmm," Noah nodded drowsily. "Tell you later."

"I'm not asleep yet." Max's voice was muffled under the cotton and wool.

Noah grinned and squeezed her. His forearm peppered with goosebumps as Rett began to draw circles on the back of his hand, light, ticklish touches, until Noah caught the fingers in his own, linking them.

All three occupants were sound asleep when the bedroom door was flung open.

George glanced at the bed and then at the open door to the left, shower and sink clearly visible. "Oh, thank God," he muttered and crossed the room in a few long strides.

Rett grunted into Noah's back. "You get used to this?"

Noah laughed, the sound husky with sleep. "Eventually."

~

WHEN GABRIEL PEERED through the cracked door midmorning, he stared, speechless. There was a small mound at the edge of the mattress that was plainly Max, pale locks of long, blonde hair spilling onto the pillow. Sprawled across the foot of the large bed was a lanky George Hix, feet dangling over the edge, his sculptured back bare and glowing in the morning light.

And lazily kissing, as though they were the only two people in the universe, much less this room or on the bed, were Noah and Rett. Gabe blushed at the quiet focus in Rett's eyes as he brushed the hair from Noah's forehead and grazed his lips along the jagged line of scars.

"Oh my God, Noah, Max is *right there*," George complained, startling Gabe when he flopped onto his back and slapped at the foot poking him in the side.

"She's asleep," Noah countered easily, closing his eyes and sighing happily when Rett began to nibble on his ear.

"Well, I'm not!" George sat up and threw his pillow at the pair. He scrubbed the sleep from his eyes and spotted Gabriel hovering just outside the door. "Hey Gabe."

"Two hundred years of isolation," Rett kissed the words into the skin under Noah's jaw. "And within twenty-four hours, not an ounce of solitude."

Noah smiled because he didn't think the words qualified anywhere near an objection.

Gabe cleared his throat. "I prepared breakfast," he said bluntly, wincing when the words echoed, too forceful and loud. He very carefully avoided looking at the foot of the bed when a tall figure stood and stretched.

And stretched.

Noah chuckled and pushed gently at Rett's shoulders, ducking under a strong arm when it tried to box him in. "Awesome. I'm hungry."

"You're always hungry," Rett and George said at the same time.

Rett smiled cautiously at Noah's brother; they had yet to have a real conversation. Which seemed rather superfluous considering they had just shared a blanket.

George gave him a wink, as if he were reading Rett's mind.

"Can everyone please shut the hell up?" Max complained, throwing the blankets off her head. "And I'm starved."

Noah clapped his hands together. "So we eat!" He grabbed Rett's face between his palms and smacked a perfunctory kiss on his lips before scooting off the bed.

Max watched the simple exchange of affection and traded glances with George.

George shrugged in response, as if to say, *Whatever makes Noah happy.*

<h1 style="text-align:center">CHAPTER 17</h1>

*N*oah shoved Rett through the bedroom door, closing and locking it behind them.

Rett ticked one eyebrow upward. "Are we hiding from someone?"

"Shhh," Noah shushed him, pressing his good ear against the door. When he heard nothing he turned with a frustrated grunt. "You were right. We have *no* privacy in this house."

"I thought you liked the presence of your family," Rett said smoothly, letting Noah pull him close.

"Not when it means I can't get you naked," Noah grumbled.

Rett's chuckle was cut off by a heated kiss.

In far too few seconds, Noah was panting with want, desire looping around them both like a physical presence; losing control had never been so easy before, nor so consciously allowed. "God, the things you do to me," he whispered.

"Not even half," Rett growled, pushing him against the door with a *thunk*. "Not even a quarter of what I'd like to."

Noah had to remind himself to breathe when Rett went to work on his neck and collarbone with a vengeance, divesting him of his t-shirt in short order.

Rett looped the chain around Noah's neck over his index finger once, twice, and pulled him off the door, backing towards the bed. "How likely are we to be interrupted in the next two hours?"

Noah swallowed. *Two hours?* "Seventy percent chance of George," he quipped lightly, hoping Rett couldn't hear the quiver in his voice.

Rett heard it; he smiled dark and sultry.

The back of his knees bumped the bed and the tags hanging from the chain around his fingers flickered in the afternoon light. "Did you know originally ID tags were circular?" he murmured, tugging on the chain again to bring Noah's mouth next to his. He brushed their lips together.

It took a moment for the words to register and Noah pulled back. "Really?"

Rett nodded unwinding the chain until Noah's identification tags nestled in his palm. He traced over the embossing with a fingertip. "The bodies of nearly half those lost in the Civil War remain unidentified today." His eyes were far away when he looked at Noah. "Something needed to be done to ensure those left behind in the aftermath did not wonder for eternity about their loved ones."

Eternity. There had been the barest of pauses before the word.

Noah ran his hands up Rett's back, soothing the troubled tension he could feel coiling beneath the golden skin. Rett may have never gone to war, but he had been left behind. "Why circular discs?" he prompted softly.

Rett shrugged lightly and gave Noah a sad smile, recognizing the question as a distraction technique but gladly accepting it. "I'm not sure. Perhaps it was a simple case of aesthetics. If I remember correctly, the round tags were initially a commercial venture that the military adopted after the turn of the century."

Noah stared. The turn of the century to Rett meant the turn of the century before the last one.

And Rett was born before the turn of the century *before that.*

"Are you all right?" Rett asked, eyes sparkling in amusement.

"Yeah," Noah breathed. "Just." He swallowed. "You've seen so much. Peace, war… all of it."

Rett inclined his head in agreement and settled the tags gently in the center of Noah's chest. He followed the movement with a kiss over Noah's heart.

Noah buried his fingers in his hair and tugged that shapely mouth back to meet his own, and if there was a hint of desperation in the way their lips moved together, neither was going to admit it, not now.

Rett allowed Noah push him onto the bed, straddling his hips and grinning down at him smugly. Rett frowned. "I don't know if I like the look on your face."

"Oh yeah?" Noah smirked. "And why is that?" He slipped the top button of Rett's pants free of its closure.

"You appear to be scheming, although without much forethought or planning if the tremble in your fingers is to be read as an indication of your nervous state."

"Shut up," Noah protested on a laugh. "I'm steady as a rock," he lied, reaching forward to cover Rett's mouth with his palm when he opened it to speak again. "And not one more criticism outta you, flyboy, or you don't get your treat."

Rett held up three fingers. *Scout's honor.*

Noah released his mouth and went to work on his pants.

"Don't call me that," Rett said first, with a glint in his eyes. "And what treat is this? I do not remember these negotiations?"

Noah shook his head, smiling at the fact that yet again Rett wasn't wearing any underwear. The man was as naked as the day he was born under these pants. Sometimes Noah's life was good. "You share historically factual firsthand tidbits with me, and I will reward you suitably for each."

Rett's eyes darkened at Noah's pretty speech pattern. "You're fucking with me."

Noah's laughter rang out loud and clear across the large room. "Don't you even dare," he warned, leaning forward and smacking a quick kiss to Rett's mouth. "And I'm not." He spread his fingers across Rett's bare chest with a happy sigh. "Now, go."

He waited as Rett studied him from under a thick curtain of black lashes.

"You enjoy war stories?" Rett finally asked.

"I'm a soldier, of course I like war stories," Noah responded dryly. His thumbs were begging to dig into the divots of Rett's hips but he restrained himself, the delay escalating his yearning as much as Rett's.

"May I touch you in this game?" Rett asked primly, hands hovering over Noah's denim-clad thighs.

"Legs only," Noah said, making up the rules as he went. He was starting to sweat.

Rett carefully considered Noah's handsome face in the light streaming through the windows. His eyes held a hint of the lush moss under the cypress by the water, and Rett remembered with a sudden, vivid clarity pulling Noah's heavy, lifeless body from the bog such a short time ago.

Noah's lips had been tinged purple from lack of oxygen, his cheeks pale and cold. The rain had pounded into both of them, a slick glossy sheen over Noah's still face, rendering his hair darker than the gold tipped strands Rett now knew.

That night, beside the rising bayou, Rett had never wanted to know the color of another's eyes more. Every cell in his body had startled to life in that instant, screaming with an oddly familiar yet impossible recognition, a claim as sure and as bold as a knight in joust for a maiden's heart.

He smiled, knowing Noah would bristle at being placed in such a passive role, even if only in Rett's romantic musings. Or maybe, he thought, revising, Noah was more aptly the enemy at the gate. Dying, breathless, heart-stoppingly beautiful, his mortality was the fault of a bitter and selfish beast, as had been the deaths of dozens of souls preceding him.

Noah's first gasping breath on Gabriel's bed, a sound more precious than any heard on this land in two hundred years, had laid siege to Rett's ironclad heart.

As Rett lowered his hands to Noah's thighs, he gladly surrendered.

"So?" Noah prodded, wiggling his butt over Rett's hips.

Rett tightened his fingers in the denim, Noah's innate sense of playful youth chasing away his melancholy. Again. "I dutifully request permission for visual assistance for my first presentation."

"I'm not getting naked yet, you perv," Noah grinned.

Rett chuckled and easily set Noah off of his lap, ignoring the accompanying grunt in protest. "Tempting, but that is not what I meant." He fastened up his pants and crossed the room to a large trunk against the wall.

Noah watched him scrounge around, long wings trailing the floor behind him, still intriguing, sleek dark feathers calling to Noah. He had a brief flash of guilt when he thought that he would hate to see them go if the curse were actually broken. *When* the curse was broken.

Rett returned, dumping an armful of yellowing newspapers circa 1944 on the bed.

Noah coughed, waving a hand in front of his face to clear the cloud. "Did you just drop a bunch of dusty old newspapers in the middle of our bed?" His toes curled at his phrasing the instant the words slipped free of his tongue.

Rett sniffed haughtily, unaware or uncaring of Noah's slip. "I did." He slid easily in place beside Noah, kissing his neck. "I thought I could read to you," he said, voice husky.

Noah closed his eyes, pulse jumping. *That voice.* "You're a cock-tease, Everett Blackburn, and you damn well know it."

"Mmmm, but I promise to make it good." He kissed Noah's neck again and pulled one of the newspapers closer, then began to read the lead story on the front page.

Noah stopped listening after the second paragraph, overcome by the graceful, melodic tones and the pretty shape of Rett's mouth as it formed the words.

Rett stopped reading after the fourth; he didn't have much choice. Noah's tongue was coaxing his own into a silky, wet dance, and there were hungry hands pulling at his skin. He did insist on gently placing the stack of newspapers on the floor before Noah rolled them to the middle of the bed.

After, as they lay nestled together, skin clammy and overheated in the humid, still day, breath mingling from mouths unwilling to stray too far from one another, Noah whispered, "I think I can pay attention now."

Rett laughed, the sound filling Noah's heart. "Later. First I'd like to tell you the story of a battle known as Operation Torch. No visuals." Rett loomed over him, a glint in his eye.

"Oh God," Noah moaned.

~

"Is your phone charged?"

"Did you charge it?" Rett asked patiently.

Noah frowned. "That's not the point."

Rett tilted his head. "If I know you have already taken care of something, why would I attempt to duplicate your efforts?"

"Don't use that fancy logic on me to try and turn my words around," Noah growled, grabbing Rett by his hips and yanking him closer.

"Should I close my eyes?" George asked dryly, forearms resting on the hood of the wrecker.

"Shut up," Noah threw over his shoulder.

"Noah, I'm fairly sure the hardware store will close at five, which means we need to get a move on. *Someone* 'napped' all afternoon," George said pointedly, air quoting for emphasis.

Noah felt the tips of his ears burn but he didn't care because George's words and easy acceptance of Rett were too welcome, too necessary. He hadn't realized how much he wanted George to be here, to share all of this, until he had shown up and been so patently *George* about everything. "Jealous?" he smirked.

"Took you long enough," George scoffed at Noah's delayed response and opened the driver's side door. "I'm getting in. Do your all fired best to gross me out and then get in the damn truck or get left behind."

Noah resisted the urge to flip him off and kept his eyes on Rett. "We won't be gone long."

"As you have already told me. Twice." Rett frowned. "Are you all right? I assure you Max will be fine here with Gabriel and I."

"No, yeah," Noah huffed. "I'm fine. I mean, you'll be fine. Hardware store, then Benny's then back. Couple hours, tops."

Rett didn't answer but pushed Noah toward the wrecker door as George turned the key and the engine roared to life. "And we will be here on your return."

Noah climbed into the passenger side and waved through the glass as they pulled away, watching the winged silhouette shrink in the mirror until it was a speck on the horizon. Something was scratching at the back of Noah's mind, a misstep, off kilter; that crazy sixth sense that had served him well all his years in a war zone, but like heck if he could figure out what it was trying to tell him now. His phone vibrated in his hand, the accompanying too cheery melody excessively loud in the quiet cab. He ignored George's teasing glance as he dialed down the volume.

Rett: *I miss the shape of your backside climbing the hill in front of me as I return to the house.*

Noah grinned. *I do have a nice ass,* he typed.

Rett: *Among other things.*

Noah: *Like my witty repartee.*

George rolled his eyes when Noah snorted a moment later.

Rett: *Did George provide assistance with that spelling?*

Noah: *No flyboy, here in the 21st century we have autocorrect. No one can spell.*

Rett: *That actually explains much about modern society.*

Rett: *And don't call me that.*

Noah typed a quick response, tilting the phone slightly away in case George happened to glance over, heart skipping at the three words before he hit send.

"I never thought I'd live to see the day," George mused without elaborating.

"Just drive, Professor," Noah ordered, but his tone was affectionate and he couldn't quite hide his smile.

CHAPTER 18

The hunter watched the creature fly over the slow-moving water of the bayou, an impossibly wide stretch of wings gliding easily across the boggy marsh. It had stood in the dusty dirt road long after the truck had disappeared around the far bend towards town.

He had seen the winged man once before; it had pulled him out from under his capsized fishing boat and left him lying on the riverbank, waiting to meet Death, heaving brackish water from his lungs. In truth, the hunter had convinced himself he had hallucinated the experience, but he had never stopped scanning the sky overhead.

And today was his lucky day.

"Rett?"

Rett turned to find Max hovering in the kitchen doorway. "Max," he smiled hesitantly, clutching a container of blue water. "Are you feeling better?"

Max's eyes slid quickly away then back, and she worried her bottom lip between her teeth. "Yeah, I'm fine. It's just," she shrugged self consciously. "Just when I wake up, you know?"

Rett nodded, his gaze falling to the floor thoughtfully. "My wife was sick every morning at six a.m. on the dot." He laughed softly. "It was a great annoyance for her."

Max crossed the kitchen, settling her back against the sink as she watched Rett slowly agitate the sediment in the bottom of the pitcher. "You had children?"

"A daughter, Emmeline." Rett shook his head. "She was very young when everything happened. Her mother—" he stopped abruptly, the words stuck in his throat.

"You don't have to tell me." Max's voice was husky when he didn't continue.

They watched the crystals dissolve as Rett continued to stir. When the whirling tornado of blue liquid slowed to a lazy spin around the glass, he tapped the wooden spoon on the lip before laying it in the sink.

"What's the water?" Max asked when the silence stretched between them unnecessarily long.

Rett palmed the bowl of the pitcher, cradling it against his stomach. "Rose food. Noah brought it from the hardware store a few days ago."

Max smiled then, a genuine fondness lighting her face. "Noah's really just a big old marshmallow. His tough exterior has always been a front."

Rett laughed quietly. "I could have used your wisdom when he first arrived."

"Did he give you a hard time?" Max leaned over onto the counter, chin in hand. "He can be a real smartass when he puts his mind to it."

"You could say that." Rett's eyes twinkled in amusement, remembering. He gestured to the back door. "Would you like to go with me? To the garden?"

"Um, sure," Max straightened with a grin. "Are we going to trade more secrets? I've been stockpiling ammunition on Noah since he found the first hairs in his pits."

Rett threw back his head and laughed and Max's breath caught in her throat. The afternoon light glinted off of the feathers on his back and the ruddy tint of his cheeks made a spectacular backdrop for the hue of his eyes. He was visually stunning, and for the briefest second, she envied Noah.

"I would love to hear more about a young Noah Hix," Rett said with a wide smile, holding the door open for her to pass.

Max proved an amiable companion as Rett fed and pruned the roses. She was highly inquisitive and charmingly sardonic, and more than once he found himself laughing out loud at her dry musings. She was currently burying her nose in the largest blossom on the bush, inhaling the lush fragrance.

"Man, roses don't smell like this anymore."

She jumped when Rett reached below her and snipped the bloom from the bush. He handed it to her with a smile. "Rett," she breathed, taken aback by the gesture. "But," she waved to the bush. "There are hardly any flowers left."

Rett pushed her hands around the stem, breaking off a stray thorn before it nicked her palm. "I want you to have it." He smiled and then bent and snipped another budless stem from the plant. "And with this, we'll try to give you a fresh root. You may take it home and plant it in the spring. Perhaps she just needs a change of scenery to find new life."

Max took the cutting from Rett, holding it gently, heart breaking at the loss and looming dread she knew were hidden in Rett's words. She threw her free arm around his neck, catching him off guard. "Thank you, Rett."

Rett quickly found his balance and accepted her hug, patting her gently on the back. "You're welcome, Max."

Max sniffed when she stepped back and swiped at her eye. "Oh God, I'm always leaking these days," she laughed. "I'm so sorry."

"You're hormonally imbalanced as your body creates a new life. There is no need for apologies. And," he said, steering her toward the house. "I find you charming."

Max snorted softly. "I'm so telling Noah you said that."

"I'd rather you didn't."

"Chickenshit."

"Absolutely."

~

"You have never had meringue like this," Noah enthused as the overhead bell tinkled.

"So just to clarify. Since you were stranded," George stepped aside to let a patron leave the diner, pink box in hand. "Have you done anything besides have sex and eat pie?"

"I'm not answering that," Noah replied with a smirk. He nodded when Maisy waved from her perch on the corner of a booth, order book in hand, pencil between her teeth.

The diner bustled with energy and smelled amazing; it looked like they had made it just in time for the dinner rush.

"You want to sit and grab a bite?" Noah asked hopefully, eyes wide and innocent.

George chuckled. "Pass. Max would murder us in our sleep." He patted Noah's back conciliatorily when his face fell. "But we can get something to go." He watched as Noah greeted no fewer than four customers by name before sliding onto a stool at the counter and waving to Benny through the cutout kitchen window. "You've been here less than two weeks."

"Yeah? So?" Noah slid him a menu across the countertop. When George raised an eyebrow, he shrugged. "Couple by the door. Madge and Dennis, married thirty-four years, raise goats. Benny buys their homemade cheese and they provide milk to a couple of families in town with lactose intolerant babies."

Noah swiveled slightly to the right. "Girl studying in the corner. Lucinda Wright. Wants to be a dentist. Raised by a single mom who works two jobs, sometimes three, just to pay their house payment after dad ran off with the checkout girl from the corner E-Z Mart. Benny feeds her dinner and she has a safe place to study while mom's working." He nodded toward the kitchen. "Speaking of, Benny, the cook, owns the diner. He's been in love with Andrea since they were fifteen. She married someone with more zeros in the bank. Joke's on her though, rich hubby drank through their cash and ran their farm into the ground. She won't leave him, but she strings Benny along anyway."

George shook his head. "You're a savant."

Noah grinned. "And waitress Maisy there," he pointed to the redhead who had waved at them when they entered. "Well, she's got it bad for Benny, because that's the way love works, George. There are no fairytales and everyone is busy looking over the proverbial fence."

"The heart wants what the heart wants," George murmured.

Noah shrugged and flipped open his menu, his earlier uneasiness creeping up his spine. "I guess." Suddenly he was less hungry and more anxious to get back to Rosewood. When a blonde waitress stopped to flirt with George while she took their order, he pulled his phone from his pocket.

Noah: At the diner, then we'll be on our way. Pie?

He didn't have to wait long for a response.

Rett: I recently found I am partial to lemon meringue and blueberry.

Rett: Mixed.

Noah smiled softly. *I recently found I'm partial to a lot of things.* His heart turned over, imagining Rett's intense gaze as he studied the small black phone, how he would smile when he read Noah's words, how the concentrated set of his mouth would firm the angles of his jaw as he composed a reply.

Rett: Me too.

Noah exhaled. *Yeah,* he thought. *Me too.*

Noah glanced around at the other diners as they ate, laughing, chatting with their neighbors. Living. Since he had left earlier in the wrecker with George, his last moments with Rett were methodically ticking away. So what the hell he was doing sitting in this diner?

He studied George's easy laughter as he teased the young waitress and wondered, for the first time in his life, what it would be like if he didn't live in the same city as his brother.

Thought, for the first time in his life, about taking something only for himself.

~

Rett was watching a strange truck slow to a stop behind the wrecker on the road when he felt the presence at his side in a flash of dizzying recognition.

It had been nearly two hundred years to the day, but there were some things one never forgot.

He turned from the window, resigned. "Apolline."

The redhead smiled slowly. "Everett." The words were a purr, rolling over her tongue in seductive tones. When she reached for his face, he drew back and she laughed. "Still playing hard to get, I see."

"What are you doing here?" Rett ground out through clenched teeth, shifting, hoping to obscure the view of the road from the bedroom window.

Noah.

"I've come to collect, angel, what do you think?" She side stepped him neatly when he tensed, leaning into the window frame and running a finger down the center pane of glass as she gazed down at the figures across the bayou. "He's quite charming."

"You will have nothing to do with Noah." Rett's words brooked no challenge.

He would die first.

Apolline smiled softly, tapping a manicured nail against the old painted wood. "Too late." When she heard Rett's wings erupt and expand behind her, she shrugged nonchalantly and turned, leaning a well-curved hip on the sill, her pastel uniform drawn snug across her lap. "You are the one who couldn't keep him occupied, my melancholy beast."

Rett's murderous glare faltered when he met her smug gaze, confused.

"Did you enjoy the pie?" she asked with a wink. Using Rett's shock as leverage, she stepped quickly into his personal space and kissed him once, hard. The cheap plastic pin of her nametag dug into his chest.

Rett shoved her back, dragging a hand across his mouth. "What do you want?" His laugh was dark, voice shaking when he spoke. "Clearly your curse is intact."

"Mmmm," she inclined her head, delicately touching her lower lip, reddened from the scrape of tooth and stubble. "Can you not feel it?" She nodded to Rett's wings. "Could you fly as far this morning as yesterday? Or the day before?"

Rett frowned, eyes narrowing on her pretty face. "What do you want?" He repeated.

"I want to make a deal," she said, dropping all pretense of flirtation, her eyes hard. "The curse weakens but it holds. And you are running out time."

"So?" Rett pulled at his hair in a sudden intense and frenzied frustration. "Do you think I don't know this? That I don't fear that man will drive away with his brother in the next few days and here I will remain? Like *this*? For all eternity? Only now, instead of backbreaking loneliness, I'm to be left with my heart shredded in pieces at my feet?"

"He loves you." Apolline's quiet words quelled his fit of pique. "In spite of both of us, all the burdens we have carried these long, lonely years, he loves you. I can see it." She contemplated Rett's handsome face. "Yet, he remains unsure and I believe it is his inner confusion that has muddied the intent of my youthful spate of sorcery."

Rett stopped, frozen in the center of a patch of sun, emotions spiking in turmoil at her confusing speech. He swallowed his unrest and forced himself closer, drawn to the odd warmth and fondness in her tone. "Why *are* you still here, Apolline? What holds you?"

A corner of her mouth lifted, sultry, and she cupped his face briefly before pulling his head down and kissing him again. When he didn't wipe her taste from his lips, she smiled sadly. "I have often wished these many years that it could have been me," she whispered.

Rett gingerly pulled her palm from his cheek. "Then it is a shame we were never lovers. Perhaps this could have been over long ago."

Apolline laughed, the sound soft and surprisingly girlish. "I never thought I'd live to see the day." She shook her head. "Nay, my heart belongs to another. As does yours." She turned back to the window. "I am fascinated by your Mr. Hix, though. How poetic, to find your heart's desire in one so clearly ill suited."

Rett joined her at the window and they watched as Noah and George talked to their guest. The trio knelt beside the river, studying its depth. Benny threw a stone and it skipped across the slow-moving water before disappearing into the weeds that lined the marsh.

"Why are you here? Now?" Rett watched her face transform when she smiled.

"Misery loves company." When she reached for him again, he leaned his cheek away and her eyes narrowed. "I was young, naïve, when I cast my first spell. And I was still quite youthful and full of hubris when I blessed you with these." She dug her fingers into the thick tuft of feathers over his shoulder and he flinched. "I didn't realize that I had tied us together, you and I, as surely as if I had cursed myself. So long as you remain thus, I remain to watch."

Rett's eyes widened in understanding. "You've been here all along."

Apolline inclined her head slightly. "In a fashion. I do possess the luxury of travel. I would have lost my mind had I been constrained to these walls and this land. My latent apologies for that, of course."

"Fuck you," Rett growled.

She smiled. "Now you're getting warmer."

Rett wrenched his shoulder from her grasp. "What do you want?" he asked again, nerves rattling in his stomach, dread weighting his bones.

"I want Benjamin Boudreau." When Rett didn't respond, Apolline flushed and she waved at the small figures on the road. "Nothing has worked, Rett. No magic, no spell, no curse. He is immune and I can only assume it is because I truly love him." Her eyes shone and in that instant Rett saw a vulnerability that surprised him. Her gaze was far away as she considered the men by the river. "I had never loved before," she trailed off.

"What has that got to do with me? Or Noah? Or this?" He gestured to the wings trailing behind him on the old wood floor.

Apolline's eyes snapped quickly to life. "I need to remove the obstacle to my affections. The one my heart desires, desires someone else. If she were gone, my path would be cleared." Her mouth thinned into a harsh line, and the effect was aging. "It has to be."

Rett waited, his trepidation so pronounced it filled his head with an anxious buzzing.

"We all have obstacles, Rett. Noah's is fear. Yours is a curse. Father Gabriel's is faith." She tapped the window again. "Benny's is the hunter who married his former lover. Mine is a girl who no longer deserves his love. The real irony is how neatly intertwined we've all become."

"I don't understand."

"I need you to be the butterfly's wing, to start the chain reaction." She shrugged. "I'm sorry, but I can see no other way. I had hoped..." she faltered and fell silent.

"And if I refuse?" But Rett already knew the answer. She didn't have to articulate it, the feeling was the same as before, a sinking sensation of despair and agonizing truth; he was going to lose in this game, and the price would be great.

"Then I will take what little power remains humming through my blood and turn Noah Hix's heart." She cocked her head. "Could you bear to know he loves another? Watch while I break him apart and spend the rest of his days tormenting his soul?"

"Noah would never be so susceptible to your darkness, not even with magic. He would never fall for your limited charms," Rett spat, but his heart raced in fear and he prayed she couldn't hear it. *Noah.* Noah, so kind and gentle, prone to nightmares, lover of cars and George and pie.

Noah, who had brought light back into this dark house, and into his life.

"You're wrong," Apolline laughed bitterly, the sound cold and dark, echoing off of the tall ceiling. "I can make anyone love me." Her eyes glittered sharply in the dim room. "Except the one I truly want."

"I will accept that risk, " he said, quietly decisive. "My answer is no." This had to end; if it meant giving up a life with Noah and spending eternity locked inside this house, these wings, so be it. He had been preparing himself to lose Noah since the moment he dragged his lifeless body from the bayou. He thought of Emmeline, her young face crumpled and tear-stained in the candlelight as her mother carried her from the house. Her cries had haunted his dreams for many years. He would never jeopardize another soul, nor destroy another heart, no matter the cost to his own fate. "I won't help you, Apolline."

"I thought you might say that," she said softly. She pointed to the far corner of the property, to the woods behind Emmeline's rose. "The hunter waits there even now, Rett. He waits for you, *wants* you. You would be his most prized trophy." Her eyes darkened, and she tilted her head thoughtfully. "A soldier, pure of heart," she whispered as she watched the men at the water's edge. Noah threw back his head and laughed, joyous, carefree, his hand on George's shoulder. "What would he do, Rett, if he thought you were in danger? How much would he sacrifice in order to save you?"

Rett sucked in a quick breath, awash in an icy resignation. "What do you want me to do?"

Apolline smiled serenely, satisfied. "Fly, Rett. I need you to fly."

CHAPTER 19

Gabriel met him at the back door. "Where are you going?" he asked, confused. "Noah's friend is still at the water, he could see you." He motioned to urge Rett back into the house.

"Gabriel, I need you to do me a favor," Rett said solemnly. His face was stony and cold, the warmth and life that had flourished and grown over the past two weeks extinguished.

Gabe's throat closed. "Rett, what is it? What happened? You're scaring me."

"I am leaving, and I will not be back." Rett clasped Gabe's hand. "You have been a good friend," he said. At the last moment, his voice caught with emotion and he had to look away. When he glanced down again his expression was cool, composed once more. "Get Noah and his family out of here, in whatever manner you can. They must never return." He squeezed Gabriel's hand. "I am sorry, old friend."

"Rett—" Gabe was cut off when Rett shoved past him and shot into the sky. "Rett!" he shouted, uncaring that Noah and the others would hear him as a feeling of helplessness and panic gripped him.

~

167

RETT KNEW the moment the hunter spotted him, the latent animal side of his senses screaming *predator.* He valiantly fought the urge to turn back to Rosewood, to safety, as he soared over the treetops, each gust of wind taking him farther from home.

He tried to blank his mind, avoid all thoughts of Noah, which proved impossible, since the only thing keeping him on course was the strength of his desire to protect the other man. Noah's voice filled his head: his banter, his laughter, his soft whispers of encouragement as they had learned all the ways they fit together. The quiet conviction when he had said *I love you.*

He would never hear that voice, those words, again.

Rett was filled with a longing so intense, he faltered, dipping too low and grazing the tips of the tree line. It was enough to destroy his carefully controlled equilibrium and he fell through the branches, limbs tearing at his chest and arms, until he landed hard on the forest floor. He lay in the woods amid the decaying rot of leaves and moss and bark, heart thudding erratically, lungs heaving, momentarily dazed. He struggled painfully to his feet, shaking the debris from his wings before he dug the phone from where he had tucked it into the waistband of his pants.

His fingers trembled as they found the letters, as he righted the only regret he had left.

I love you. I should have told you.

He pressed the tiny arrow and then took to the skies.

NOAH HEARD the tinny echo of Gabe's shout and saw the dark figure streak across the sky.

"What the?" Benny exhaled, shading his eyes with one hand. "What the hell was that?"

Noah glanced at George, expression grim. "I think we'll have to talk barges and backhoes another time, Benny, but thanks for coming out to check the crossing for us."

Benny turned to Noah with a wry expression. "Nice try, brother, but a man just flew over your house."

Noah opened his mouth to protest when George interrupted.

"You've seen him before." George nodded when Benny didn't deny it. "I think probably most of you have seen him before, am I right?"

"What?" Noah looked between the men, confused. "Why didn't you say anything?"

Benny chuckled. "And risk sounding like a lunatic to the first decent crawfish gigger I've had the pleasure to meet in years?"

Noah huffed a laugh, relief at Benny's confession mingling with the heavy concern settling in his belly. *Where was Rett going?* "Who else?"

Benny shrugged. "Most people, I 'spect. At least those who live round these parts. This house," his eyes were misty as they surveyed the old mansion, its whitewashed walls turned pink from the setting sun. "It's got some magic about it, don't it?"

Noah didn't answer, because it wasn't really a question. "Benny," he began but the other man held up a hand.

"Mind my own business and nevermind my romantic musings, so you can go after your friend. Is that about right?"

"Thanks, man," Noah said, accepting the strong handshake that followed Benny's words. "Call you tomorrow?"

If he had turned two seconds sooner, if Benny hadn't cocked his head at a sound Noah couldn't hear, they might have missed the movement of the hunter in the woods.

Noah's eyes followed the outline of a man as he disappeared into the thick brush. His heart stopped when the red-gold light of the sun flashed off the narrow object he held pointed at the sky: the barrel of a gun. Noah reached blindly for his brother; younger, steadier, the reason Noah had gotten up in the morning for the majority of his life. "George."

"Hang on," George murmured, gripping Noah's shoulder hard enough to burn. "Gabe's coming."

The former priest was running, and had Noah's heart not been lodged in his throat, choking every emotion but fear from his body, he might have laughed at his uncoordinated form. Gabe stumbled once in the thick grasses, and then once again before he reached the edge of the bayou, red-faced and out of breath. He started when Max appeared at his side seconds later, having followed him from the house when she heard his shout.

"Rett," he managed to gasp before he coughed, long and deep.

"Where did he go?" Noah asked, desperation making his tone harsher than he intended.

"He said goodbye." Gabe's face filled with anguish and he was unable to continue. Max threw her arms around him, meeting Noah's gaze over the slow moving, murky water.

"It was a woman, she had red hair. She was there with him in the bedroom, and then suddenly she wasn't." Max bit her lip, eyes troubled. "She threatened him. With you."

"Who was she?" Noah frowned. "I don't understand!" He shrugged George's hand off his shoulder and stalked to the water's edge. "Gabe, so help me God. Rett's life is in danger." He jabbed his finger at the woods. "A hunter just spotted him, and he didn't seem at all surprised by what he was seeing. Pull yourself together!"

"Apolline," Gabe whispered, looking at Max with respect. "Where were you?"

Noah turned to George with a clenched jaw. "What's he saying?"

"A name, I think," George said. "Now he's asking Max where she was hiding."

Noah scoffed and yelled over the marsh. "Max could work for the goddamn CIA, padre! You've never met anyone better at eavesdropping in your entire life."

"Then we need her over here," Benny interrupted. "How do we do that?"

"You can't," Gabe said, shaking his head, strangely calmed after Max had recounted the overheard exchange. "You don't have time. What day is it?"

"October thirteenth," George offered. Noah bristled beside him in impatience.

"Two hundred years," Gabe whispered, letting the misery of a long ago night sweep through him, accepting the pain gladly, because it was almost over. He took a deep breath and focused on the one among them who possessed the power to obliterate a curse. "What would you do to save him?" He repeated Apolline's words.

Noah didn't hesitate. "Everything."

Gabe nodded. "The hunter was part of a trap. It involves you, Benjamin Boudreau."

"Me?" Benny's eyes widened in shock. "I…" He faltered and Noah saw the moment recognition filtered across his face.

"Who was it?" Noah urged, abandoning the swamp's edge. George read his mind and dug the wrecker keys from his pocket.

"Andrea's husband," Benny said slowly, remorse tingeing his words. He knew Noah would recognize the cruelty the man was capable of. "His land borders the woods."

"Let's go." Noah was already stalking toward Benny's truck.

"Noah!" Gabe shouted. "You bring him back!"

Noah didn't answer, meeting George's eyes with determination. "What do you have in the truck?"

"A twenty-two," George said apologetically. "Half a box of shells."

"Get 'em. It'll have to do." He looked at Benny, expression dark, anger coloring his cheeks. "You're driving."

RETT CIRCLED THE FARMHOUSE, staying low to afford himself some camouflage. He knew the hunter had fallen behind; his back and neck no longer prickled with the instinct to run. That wouldn't last.

He scanned the grounds for Apolline but saw nothing; the woods were still.

Too still.

The air hung heavy and moist, a tangible thing, and without a breeze the scent of the nearby swamp was thick. Not a cricket nor cicada chirped in the waning light of dusk; no evening predators stirred to life in the forest, preparing for the night's hunt.

There was only one predator in the forest tonight, and Rett understood that he was the prey.

A surge of anger flooded his system and he descended silently, dropping to his feet amid the soft rot of the woodland floor. It was likely futile, but he was not going to make himself an easy target. If Apolline wanted to play, using Rett and Noah, Benny, Gabe—all of them—as pawns, then he could at least make it a challenge. He tucked his wings tight against his back and sank into the deep shadows to wait.

～

GABE'S EYES were a little wild when he grabbed Max by the shoulders and gave her a little shake. "What else? What else did she say?"

"Gabe," Max said quietly, gripping his forearms, trying to diffuse his frenzy before he lost all composure.

Gabe's face cleared and he realized his nails were digging into the soft skin of her arms, would probably bruise. He dropped his hands and flushed. "I'm sorry."

"It's okay," Max soothed. "Now think. We have to figure out what Apolline meant."

Gabe reached for her hand and turned toward the house, his face settling into firm resolution. "I already know what she meant. The curse is failing."

Max had to lengthen her stride to keep up. "But Rett still has wings."

Gabe shrugged. "And I have a cold. Do you know in two hundred years I have never once been sick? Not even a sneeze?" They ran up the marble steps, and Gabe had a flash of memory so clear he stumbled. He had once stood in this exact spot and watched his life become a fable. "Tell me again."

"The hunter wants Rett, and she wants Benny, and somehow it's all connected."

Gabe paused at the threshold, frowning. "Apolline is in love," he said slowly. "She has a weakness."

"She said your weakness was faith," Max replied softly.

Gabe snorted and pulled Max through the doorway. "Not today it's not."

THE MELODIC PEAL of a text message echoed in the cab, startling the occupants. Dust flew up behind them in whorls of dusky orange and tan, obliterating the landscape in the rearview mirror as they tore down the dirt road toward the neighboring farm.

Noah dug the cheap phone from his front pocket, hands shaking more than he liked as he read the message. He was filled instantly with rage, heart blackened by fear and pending loss, and he gripped the device so tightly it dug into his palm.

"It's not over yet," George said quietly, covering the hand holding the phone. When Noah didn't move or respond, George squeezed. "Noah. It's not over. Tell him."

Noah breathed slowly in and out through his nose, eyes burning, ears ringing. The phantom tone that had haunted him for years, mocking the absence of sound, grew until his vision swam. Stuck between two people, one his oldest and best friend, the other his newest, Noah had nowhere to hide from his feelings in the small cab. Nowhere to gather his thoughts. If these were to be his last words to Rett, he wanted to choose carefully, only the best words, the words of his heart. But there was no space here, no room to expose the secret truth of *Noah Hix,* the truth that Rett had found so easily and urged to the surface with every hard won smile or cherished touch.

It was baring his soul with no guarantees, walking into battle with no promise of victory.

He began to type as a ragged farmhouse appeared on the horizon.

CHAPTER 20

*R*ett had no idea what to expect as he stalked in concentric circles, closer and closer to the farm. His senses had picked up on the presence of the farmer a few moments before, but he had yet to spot him. There was still no sign of Apolline. In the distance he could hear a vehicle on the road, driving too fast, dirt billowing both ahead and behind and filling the sky above the farmhouse with a thick, brown fog of dust.

He wondered—

A twig snapped under a heavy boot to his right and he hurled himself into the air, no updraft to provide buoyancy for the thick undercarriage of feathers, the tightly packed trees offering little room to expand his wings.

He never noticed the small plastic rectangle fall from his waistband and into the leaves.

It was more a giant leap than a true flight, and when he landed in the shadows of the treeline, just shy of the yard, Rett was confronted with a shocking vision: himself, standing with wings outstretched at the edge of the sagging, broken steps of the sad little house.

The hunter and the truck emerged from the clog of dirt road dust in the same instant.

The gun was raised and leveled, synchronized, in time with the strong body that launched itself from the still moving truck.

Before he heard the crack of gunfire, Rett understood Apolline's folly. He prayed to a God he no longer believed in that she was here to see it, even as his head, the forest, his very soul flooded with the impact of the curse disintegrating, breaking him apart, from the inside out.

Win this heart with love and compassion and grace...

Love is a temporary insanity.

Sometimes your heart chooses for you.

The one my heart desires, desires someone else...

Rett fell to his knees amid the leaves and moss and stones, powerless, as the only one to ever find him worthy threw himself in front of a bullet to save his wretched, undeserving life.

I recently found I'm partial to a lot of things.

In that instant, Rett knew true despair: the moment Noah Hix walked into his life, the curse had been doomed to fail. But Rett had penance yet to pay.

"SHOULDN'T we be trying to find a way across the river? We're stuck!" Max was starting to panic. Gabe's unusually stark expression was scaring her and his mumblings about curses and witches had cooled the very blood in her veins. She rubbed her arms as a chill ran through her.

"We're not stuck," Gabe replied, pulling an old leather bound book from the bottom of the trunk in Rett's bedroom. When he opened the dusty tome, he smiled grimly at the messily restrung rosary that held an oft-read position between the pages. "I didn't only study carpentry and gardening for the past two hundred years."

Max shivered at the macabre etchings on the yellowed paper. In her hands she held the fading pink rose Rett had given her. It's scent was still lovely, but the petals were wilting fast, and she instinctively feared the symbolism of its rapid decline.

Gabe slammed the trunk closed and hurried Max from the room and down the steps, crossing the marble foyer and porch, descending to the worn grass of the yard, as near as he could remember to the exact spot where Rett had fallen all those years ago. "Do you have the rose?" he asked dumbly, suffering a fit of nerves, and Max nodded, handing it to him. He shook his head. "No, Max. This has to be you. We need all the magic we can get if this is going to work. And you, my girl, are a walking, breathing miracle."

"I can't do it," Max hiccupped in a fresh wave of panic, the first bright tear snaking down her flushed cheek.

"Yes you can," Gabe said fiercely, gripping her arms and squeezing her tight. "I have faith in you, too, Maxine."

He pressed the rosary and the book into her hands and stepped away.

After a deep, shuddering breath, Max began to chant.

Years ago, in his first months in the desert, Noah's unit had been ambushed as they slept. He had been torn from his restless dreams of home by the sooty taste of gunpowder and the coppery smell of blood.

Although it would be years before he would ultimately lose half of his hearing, on that cold, horrific night, Noah had heard nothing at all, that singularly vital sense failing him when he could have used it the most. He had run from his tent, scrabbling his night vision goggles into place, hands shaking too hard to position his gun. Not even his worst nightmares could have prepared him for this.

Bodies of his friends littered the ground. Through the smoky haze of fire and gun reports, his visual acuity honed in on the enemy figures who had snuck into their midst, who had used the advantage of darkness and chaos to lay waste to their camp. Absent of sound, the tableau of battle became a rich medley of sight and smell and taste. In one brief, astonishing flash of power, when it seemed all hope had been lost, Noah's unit had turned the tide.

Something had pulsed through the camp in a rolling ripple, a psychic connection between a brotherhood forged in countless hours of training and shared misery. Noah couldn't see or hear his teammates, but he had instinctively *known* where they were, and it had been that connection that had ultimately allowed them to gain the upper hand.

It had been unexplainable, a force unrecognizable and never spoken of again.

Magical.

Miraculous.

That night, Noah had accepted there were things in the universe he was not meant to understand.

As he dove from Benny's truck, Noah never heard the sharp crack that split the night air. Not that it would have made any difference. He had one goal, and in that instant, nothing else mattered.

He saw a figure at the periphery of the yard as the slug tore through his chest and drove him into the hard-packed earth. That body crumpled in tandem with his own, and they hit the ground together in a flash of brilliant light that swept through the clearing in a soundless wave.

Noah knew that ripple. He closed his eyes and smiled.

A woman's hysterical screams were the first thing he heard when time sped up and the world found its axis again.

"Noah!"

That was George. And the hands pressing too hard on the fiery wound in his chest must belong to George too. Noah fought to stay awake, spotted a faded floral housedress on the ground beside his head, the scuffed toes of Benny's boots as he cradled a woman in his arms.

Andrea.

Noah felt his consciousness wane.

"Noah. Noah! Stay with me," George urged. He slapped Noah's cheek until he saw his brother's vision clear.

"Rett," Noah whispered.

George ripped his shirt off and balled it up, shoving it against the rapidly-growing red stain on Noah's chest. "I don't know. It," George shook his head grimly. "It was Rett. And then it wasn't."

"Apolline," Noah mouthed. "Curse." His heart clenched hard and he would have doubled over in pain if he could move. He wondered if it was because the organ was fighting to pump its last beats or if his heart knew something his brain wasn't yet allowing him to see.

What happened to a creature more than two hundred years old when time's clock began to tick again?

WHEN HIS KNEES hit the ground, rocks bit into his tender skin and Rett nearly smiled. *Pain.* It had been a long time since he had suffered something so simple and pure. Belatedly, he thrust out his wings to break his fall, confused when first his palms and then his shoulder thudded against the decaying leaves.

The wings were gone.

He was unsure if it was George's horrified shout, or an enraged shriek he recognized as Apolline, that finally spurred him to his feet. He struggled to find balance without the heavy appendages weighting him down. He was light. Free. As he lurched across the yard, finding a forgotten rhythm, he knew the moment she spotted him, a telltale patch of scarlet through the trees as she shoved the dazed hunter aside and ripped the gun from his hands.

And still he ran.

Benny's shout of warning was cut off when a dark shadow fell across the yard.

The ground shook from the force of the impact as the creature landed directly in Apolline's path, huge golden brown wings providing a protective shield between she and Rett.

Gabriel took the first bullet square in the chest. He advanced, smiling when the second struck him. Apolline's gaze faltered, unsure. She began to back away from the imposing figure of the former priest until her back hit the trunk of a tree.

They both ignored the hunter as he scrambled away, disappearing into the brush.

Apolline screamed in rage. "What have you done?" She swung the butt of the gun at his head and Gabe caught her wrist.

"I am ending this once and for all," he said, voice strong, breaking over the peaceful night with a latent power. He yanked the gun from her hand and easily bent it in half.

Apolline blanched when she looked over Gabe's shoulder and saw the fear and loathing on Benny's face, his arms still cradling an old lover. It was though a string had been pulled, releasing the power from her veins, and she sank to her knees in defeat.

Rett dropped beside Noah in the grass, hands running over his arms, his shoulder, skirting the would. He cupped his jaw and gently turned his face. "What have you done?" he asked miserably, throat burning, chest taut with fear.

"It was my turn," Noah whispered, breath rattling in his chest. He coughed and the sound was too wet, too thick. "How'd I do?"

"I would kill you myself if I didn't love you so damn much," Rett managed, fury and fear and relief all wrapped up in an exasperated tangle of love so deep and encompassing it took his breath away. He pushed George's hands away to inspect the wound, lifting the makeshift bandage that covered the neat hole of the entrance wound. A quick brush of his palm across Noah's back revealed no torn flesh to indicate an exit.

Noah grinned weakly, reading the fear and wanting nothing more than to vanquish it. If the fuzzy edges around his vision and the slowing thud of his pulse were anything to go by, he didn't have a lot of time. "Kiss me, stupid. I just saved your fake life."

Rett huffed but obliged, a salty, soft brush against Noah's dry lips before he glanced up as he felt Gabe's approach. The priest was a vision, his new form vibrating with power and light.

George stared. "Holy shit."

Max raced into the clearing, thrashing through brush and limbs as she escaped the cover of the woods. "I thought you were going to give me the all clear?" she complained, panting and out of breath. She grinned when she saw George's expression.

"I was going to," Gabe insisted. He ruffled his feathers self-consciously.

"Apolline?"

Gabe glanced back at the tree line, but the woman had disappeared. "Powerless. And apparently missing."

"That was my waitress," Benny said, finding his voice. "My waitress was, is," his mouth snapped shut. "What the fuck just happened?"

Noah began to cough, cutting off any attempt at explanation. His eyes fluttered closed.

"Noah? Noah, come on, stay with me," Rett pleaded, patting his pale cheeks. "Don't you dare leave me now. I don't want to do this by myself."

Noah groaned and blinked slowly. "Stop smacking me," he rasped. "Do what?"

Rett exhaled in a rush and kissed him hard. "Be human. And don't do that again."

"I'll call an ambulance," George said, belatedly remembering the phone in his pocket. He flushed, anxiety suffusing him as Noah struggled to remain conscious, fingers clumsy as he tried to dial.

"How far is the nearest doctor?" Rett asked.

"There's a county ambulance service about thirty miles south. The closest hospital is a little farther," Benny answered grimly.

"We'll have to drive him," George said, scrambling to his feet. "Benny."

Andrea backed away from the group, shaking and confused. Benny reached for her and she shrank from his touch. "Where's my husband?" she whispered and Benny's face hardened.

Even after the man had pointed a gun at her, had shot an unarmed man, still she pined for him.

Benny's hand fell to his side and he mentally closed the pages of a long overdue book.

"I'll pull up the truck. Andrea, bring all the towels you can spare. And bottled water if you've got it."

Andrea hesitated and Benny snarled, "Go!"

Gabe knelt beside Rett, a hand on his old friends back, the skin smooth and unblemished, pale from decades hidden from the sun. He reached down and touched Noah's cheek, wondering—

Nothing happened.

Rett looked at him in confusion. "What are you doing?"

Gabe shrugged. "Thought it was worth a shot." He glanced at George regretfully. "I must be out of magic."

"You did well, Father," Rett said quietly, not taking his eyes from the uneven rise and fall of Noah's chest. "You saved my life, and I will forever be in your debt."

Gabe flushed and nodded, smiling at Max. "I had help."

The crunch of gravel drew their gaze and an unmarked sedan nosed between the trees, a single light flashing on the dash.

"Sonofabitch," George breathed.

"Tyler?" Max said in surprise, jumping to her feet.

A man climbed from the driver's side and stalked across the yard, mouth downturned in a grim line.

Gabe unconsciously shifted in front of George, who grinned down at him.

Tyler slapped a sheaf of papers against Max's chest and scowled at the man lying on the ground. "Why is it always you three and a body?"

Max read the first line on the top page and bit her lip with a watery smile.

The angry set of Tyler's jaw softened at her expression.

Rett cleared his throat. "How fast is that car?"

Tyler dragged his gaze from Max and knelt beside Noah, dark fingers going to the pulse in his wrist before he peeled back the shirt to inspect the wound. "Fast enough. Watch his head." It was all the warning Rett had before Tyler lifted Noah's limp body in his arms and was striding toward the car.

"How the hell did you find us?" George asked, sliding into the front seat after Max, accepting the water and towels from Benny through the open door. Rett was ensconced on the back seat, cradling Noah's head in his lap. He motioned for a towel and George passed him two, wincing when he saw the bright red stain of Rett's palms.

Tyler started the car and slammed his door. "I pegged Max's phone a couple of months ago." He flipped the switch on the siren and the sound pealed through the night air as he made a u-turn in the yard.

"You lowjacked me?" Max asked, incensed.

"Damn straight," Tyler said under his breath. Max opened her mouth to protest and Tyler calmly took her hand. "For once in your damn life, Maxine, shut up."

In spite of herself, Max grinned and nodded.

George handed a phone through the window to a hovering and unsure Gabriel. "I'll keep you updated." He frowned at Gabe's grimace. "You do know how to use a cell phone, right?"

"I'll show him the ropes," Benny said, pulling on Gabe's arm to move his wings a safe distance as Tyler rammed the pedal to the floor.

As the card sped away, Benny and Gabe were quiet, each lost in their thoughts.

"You want a ride?" Benny finally asked, gesturing at his truck.

"I was just about to ask you the same thing," Gabe said solemnly.

Benny snorted, which made Gabe grin, until both men were laughing, the absurdity of the day begging for release.

"How 'bout I drive this time, and you tell me about my waitress Maisy and all the trouble she's been causing."

Gabe frowned. "The drive is not that long."

Benny chuckled and shook his head. "You can give me the cliff notes version."

Gabe was still trying to figure out who *Cliff* was when they pulled onto the road.

CHAPTER 21

*R*ett was wearing pale teal scrubs and mainlining stale coffee. He was also pacing a hole in the floor.

George watched him walk back and forth in front of the vending machines, surgical booties the only coverings on his feet, and marveled tiredly at how quickly the other man had adapted to being entirely human again. Max had been the one who had begged the clothing for him from an orderly; George had been too beside himself with worry after the surgical team whisked his brother through a set of swinging doors. Noah's skin had been as pasty as the sheets that covered his gurney.

"Mr. Hix?"

George stood, heart falling into his stomach as he faced the surgeon. If Max hadn't grabbed his hand, he didn't know if he could have remained on his feet.

The doctor studied the mismatched group, Rett hovering silently behind George, Tyler's empty shoulder holster still belted firmly in place. "He's going to be okay."

George blew out the breath he'd been holding. "How is he? Did you get the bullet?"

The doctor hesitated. His white lab coat hung loose around his thin frame, the ties of his mask looped over his ears. He appeared simultaneously impossibly young and old beyond his years. His eyes were tired and wary as they regarded George, but he gentled his voice. "We couldn't remove it. It's lodged in his heart, but miraculously, there's no bleeding, no tears." He paused and scratched his head. "It's the damnedest thing I've ever seen. That any of us have ever seen. It's like it just…stopped."

Max squeezed George's hand when he tensed. "Is it dangerous?"

The doctor shook his head, remorse on his face. "I'm sorry, but if we try to remove it, we would most assuredly kill him. It's almost perfectly positioned in the only inch in the heart it could possibly rest and not affect function." He cleared his throat. "If it moves, it will probably kill him instantly."

"Oh my God," Max whispered and reached behind her for Tyler who appeared immediately at her side.

"But there's nothing to say that it ever will," the doctor assured them. "He'll recover from the minor surgery required to stitch him up and then, for all intents and purposes, be as good as new."

"But," George began, stopping when the doctor held up a hand.

"Today is the day you start believing in miracles, Mr. Hix. I know I just did." He nodded once and strode back through the swinging doors, disappearing in a flash of jade green and white.

"He's going to be okay," Rett said softly.

George turned, huffing a laugh when Rett swayed on his feet, nearly face planting on the tile. "Hold on there, cowboy. You might have OD'd on crappy caffeine."

"I can see him?"

"Yeah. As soon as they put him in a room, Rett, you can see him." George's smile was wide and infectious. "Holy shit, Rett. We did it! We broke the curse!"

Rett grinned weakly as George and Max began to laugh, dancing a little jig around him in the waiting room.

Tyler watched them, eyebrows drawn together in a confused frown. "What curse?" he finally asked.

Max laughed. "Oh brother. Have I got a story for you."

"Does it involve cheeseburgers? Because I'm starved," Tyler complained, puling her close and watching her mouth lift at the corners in a happy smile.

"I'm pregnant," she said bluntly.

"Aw, fuck," George clapped a palm over his eyes.

Max's gaze narrowed on Tyler's handsome face as she waited for him to respond.

He blinked. "Then I guess it's a damn good thing I got divorced."

Max smacked him in the shoulder. "Ass."

Tyler grinned, wrestling for control until he had her tucked in the circle of his arms. "Daddy," he corrected. "Jesus," he breathed, eyes glassy as a delayed reaction took hold. "Oh Jesus."

"Chair," George warned and Rett pushed an empty one toward the man.

In the end, Max went to buy the cheeseburgers while Tyler sat with his head between his knees.

It was in the early hours after midnight before Rett was allowed into Noah's room. He refused to leave his side after that.

Noah was released late the next day, and when the group arrived at Rosewood it was to discover the narrow crossing was passable at last. And that the resident former priest was back to his normal body shape and type. Max high-fived him for the success of their joint magical effort.

BEFORE HE WENT TO BED, George stuck his head in Rett's bedroom. "You asleep?"

"I would be if everyone would stop popping in to ask me that," Noah said grumpily. "Where's Rett?"

"Where do you think?" George grinned, crossing the room and sitting gingerly on the edge of the bed.

Noah rolled his eyes. "With Max? I'd be jealous if she didn't have that smug bastard sniffing at her heels."

George raised his eyebrows as someone behind him cleared his throat.

"That smug bastard is right behind you, isn't he?" Noah closed his eyes in resignation. He never could catch a break.

"Just wanted to say good night," Tyler said cheerfully.

"Yeah, good night." Noah blew him a little kiss which Tyler ignored.

"You ever going to cut him some slack?" George asked, amused.

"Nope." Noah winced when he went to tuck his arms behind his head. *Arms above head equals bad idea.*

"Hey, you know how you asked me to look up Rett's daughter? See if I could find out what happened to her?"

Noah stared at his stupidly smart baby brother. "That was like one day ago. You can't possibly have found out anything in *one day.*"

George chuckled. "It's the twenty-first century, Noah. With the internet, anything is possible."

Noah started to sit up and George pushed him back onto the pillows. He huffed in frustration, glancing at the cracked door. "So did you find something or not?"

George nodded, eyes sparkling mischievously. "Oh I found something. You're just not going to believe it."

"Wow, George, can you save the lecture for Father Gabe? He probably gets off on that professor schtick."

"Very funny," George said drily, but his neck flushed. "I found a record of Emmeline Blackburn, who left New Orleans, and visited her relative for a time in England—Mary Godwin."

"So she survived."

"Noah, Mary Godwin later married Percy Shelley." At Noah's blank look George huffed. "Noah. Mary Shelley."

Noah shook his head, although a spark of some distant cell of familiarity—

"Oh my God, Noah. Mary Shelley wrote Frankenstein!"

Noah's eyes widened and his gaze flew to the door, where he could hear Rett's deep voice as he climbed the staircase, followed by Max's sweet chuckle. He caught the faintest swath of bright pink as Rett passed her what was likely a rose, just outside the door. He grinned. Rett was probably boring her to death with an explanation of plant rot or aphids. "Part man," he murmured, then looked back at his brother. "Nah. Come on, George."

George shrugged. "I guess we'll never know. But it seems pretty odd, don't you think? The daughter of a monster, spends time with a woman who writes *the* definitive horror novel? About a man made of different parts?"

"My boyfriend is Frankenstein," Noah said slowly.

"Your boyfriend, huh?" George smiled when Noah blushed but didn't deny it.

"Crazy, right?"

George watched Noah, content in the realization that his brother was safe, and happy. Possibly for the first time in his life "Surprisingly, it's not." He shrugged at Noah's doubtful expression. "What? It's not. He fits."

TYLER AND MAX left Louisiana first, then Gabriel and George in the wrecker a few days later. A flush of fluids and replacement of fuses and filters, and the Road Runner had started up with a purr as soon as George funneled in fresh gas.

One last goodbye dinner and pie at Benny's, with a promise to stay in touch, and then it was their last night on the bayou.

"What do you think happened to her?" Noah wondered, admiring the curve of Rett's bare shoulder as he stripped off his t-shirt.

"Apolline?" Rett kicked off his jeans and and then his boxers too, grinning at Noah's raised eyebrows. "I don't know. Gabriel was pretty sure he effectively drained her power with the counter spell. I suppose we'll have to wait and see if she ever reappears."

Noah frowned. "I don't really like the wait and see approach."

Rett settled over him on the bed, sighing contentedly at the first contact of skin on skin. "Mmmm," he hummed noncommittally.

"Sort of like how you feel about this bullet." Noah gingerly touched his bandage.

Rett's face fell. "Noah—"

"I'm sorry," Noah rushed to soothe him. He kissed Rett hard, wrapping his arms around him. "I'm sorry," he said again.

Rett covered his mouth with his hand. "I love you."

Noah smiled behind the palm before he dragged it from his face. "Yeah, just don't forget who said it first." Rett's expression grew distant, something it had done with regularity throughout the day as they had packed his belongings. "Are you sure you want to leave?" Noah murmured.

"I want to be wherever you are."

The words were delivered so solemnly resolute that Noah's heart clenched tight in his chest and he said a quick prayer that that damn bullet stayed put.

"Yeah, me too," he said softly, pulling him close for a kiss. He ran his hands down Rett's back, thrilling at the smooth warmth of the muscles clenching under his fingertips. "Not gonna lie," he confessed in a whisper. "I might miss them a little."

Rett snorted lightly. "I'll miss the way you loved them."

"This is good too," Noah breathed, digging his nails into the sensitive skin over Rett's scapula, then sliding around to cup his chin. "Oh man, this is going to sound weird."

"What?" Rett asked, kissing Noah's hand when it passed over his lips. "What is it?"

"You." Noah rolled them over, dipping his head to kiss the hollow of Rett's throat. "In *clothes*," he chuckled, husky and deep. "Fitted button down." He nibbled on a delicate collar bone. "Suspenders."

Rett sighed, threading his fingers through Noah's hair.

Noah shifted lower, pressing open lips to Rett's sternum. "Waistcoat," he whispered, mouth widening in a smile when he glanced up to see how Rett was faring.

Rett's eyes were dark, hot, and he bit his lip as he tightened his grip on Noah's neck. "Anything else?" he asked tightly.

"Mmmm," Noah exhaled into his skin, dragging his mouth across the ridge of his ribcage, into the divot of his hip. "My jeans," he said around a mouthful of warm skin. "My old t-shirts."

"Noah." Rett tensed when Noah's mouth hovered over his hipbone.

Noah suddenly laughed, resting his forehead on Rett's stomach, shoulders shaking with amusement.

"What?" Rett asked in consternation, smiling in spite of his state of arousal and Noah's proximity to the place he most wanted that pretty mouth. "Noah."

"I'm hornier than hell because I want to take you *shopping,*" Noah lifted his head, eyes twinkling.

"That's a…first?" Rett smiled, grazing Noah's jaw with his knuckles. He cupped his handsome face and pulled gently, urging him up his body.

Noah obliged, breathing the air between them with each soft kiss. "That's a first," he finally said in affirmation.

"Noah," Rett moaned when hands swept under him to graze the sensitive skin bracketing his spine.

Noah smiled into his throat, the great dark wings a near tangible thing, their scent, their texture, the responsive way Rett reacted to his touch. Maybe he could still feel them too.

Thank you, he thought.

AT THE CORNER of the moonlit yard, behind a curtain of Spanish moss and cypress stood a lone figure. She balanced atop a ledge of native stone, hovering over the swampy water of the bayou.

Apolline smiled up at the bedroom window.

"You're welcome."

EPILOGUE

They bought a little house outside of Kansas City, a tiny two bedroom cottage with whitewashed stucco walls and a steeply peaked roof. It faced the east and the morning sun would greet the square parcel of land each and every day, rising over the far hillside and bathing the little house in a golden glow.

Usually Rett was waiting for it, tending the roses that lined the fence, their heirloom fragrance filling the air.

Noah would find him, shears in hand, standing barefoot and shirtless in the dewy morning grass, eyes closed and face lifted to the skies.

Remembering.

Noah would wrap his arms around him, offer a sip from a steaming mug to chase the chill from Rett's bones. There would be birds in the spring and summer, their sweet melody breaking across the quiet country lane that led down to the road, and then on to town.

Rett would welcome the coffee, and the embrace, and the birdsong and the sun, and sometimes he would coax Noah back into their cozy bedroom, persuade him to go to work a little later than the norm.

Rett would name all of the woodland animals that visited their yard, funny, long-forgotten monikers from his earliest memories, although the squirrels were always Earl, Jr. Eventually they were joined in the little house by an oversized dog of mixed pedigree and a fat tabby cat of questionable disposition.

Still later, a horse would be added to their menagerie and Rett would one day teach their niece, Claire, to ride. Claire, in turn, would teach Rett about everything Noah had forgotten by becoming an adult, like the joy of finding the prize in the bottom of a Cracker Jacks box and sleeping in a tent under the stars and the cool thrill of an orange push-pop in the summer.

There would be a period in which they would long for a child of their own, but fate would never smile that blessing upon them. Still, they were happy and content, and when George and his wife became parents of a precious baby named Lucas, Noah and Rett would spoil the boy as though he were their own.

One day far into the future, and with Gabe's blessing, Noah would convince Rett to write down his story, and one day farther still, they would receive a brown, paper-wrapped package in the mail: Rett's first book, his named carved into the tooled leather cover in gold. It was met with mixed reviews and a modicum of success, the most common complaint being that the story was too fantastical, that such magic could never exist in a world such as this.

But critics had only to venture up the country lane to understand the simple charm and truth behind Rett's words, to find the magic that lived on and on in the little house. It had traveled with these two hearts over the miles between the bayou and the prairie, enveloping them as they left behind the lives they had known apart and embraced a new one, together.

It would survive all the days they would spend in the little house, cherished moments alone, and others spent with family and friends. It would survive a niece and nephew's childhood, and on and on and on, until those children brought their own children to listen to Uncle Rett tell the tale of the winged beast in the castle and the crocodile named Earl.

It would survive until a long forgotten slug would finally wind its way loose in the middle of a cold, winter's night and stop a heartbeat so dearly loved.

And its echo could still be felt when the pair were found together, locked in an eternal slumber, Rett's heart having ceased in the same moment, forever in sync with Noah's.

George would say it couldn't bear the thought of beating alone.

They were buried together as snow clouds gathered in the distance. The flakes would hold off until after the service, beginning to fall as the last car left the lot and blanketing the world in a soft cover of white. In the spring, Max would plant a cutting from Emmeline's rose, and for years the blooms would draw many a visitor to the simple headstone that marked their grave.

They would come to admire the beautiful color and fragrance of the flowers, but would stay in thoughtful contemplation of the inscription on the stone, taken from the dedication of Rett's book.

Magic need not be fleeting nor transient.
It doesn't play favorites or cast stones.
It exists in a rainbow, in a caterpillar, in a bumblebee.
Magic exists in a newborn's first smile and in the perfect cup of coffee.
There is magic enough for everyone, if you know where to find it.
Once upon a time, magic bound two unlikely hearts.
And together, they found forever.

ABOUT THE AUTHOR

AJ Lange is an Amazon best-selling author of male/male romance and mystery. She lives deep in the Southern Plains and when she's not devising new ways to describe pectorals, she watercolors, reads, and naps.

She spends way too much time looking up at the stars.

Find her on Patreon at patreon.com/ajlange or join her mailing list to keep in touch!

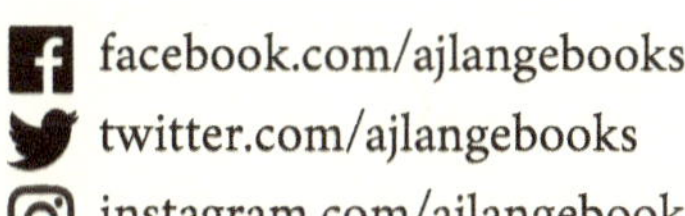

facebook.com/ajlangebooks
twitter.com/ajlangebooks
instagram.com/ajlangebooks

ALSO BY AJ LANGE

Freefall

Past, Present

Small Town Charmer

Lost Souls

Unlimited Potential

Short Stories

Exposure

Cinderfella

No Strings

Baker's Dozen

www.ingramcontent.com/pod-product-compliance
Lightning Source LLC
Chambersburg PA
CBHW031040160726
47991CB00005B/1967